A PONY FOR TWO

A PONY FOR TWO

OTHER BOOKS IN
THE PONY CLUB LIBRARY INCLUDE

PONY CLUB CAMP
PONY CLUB TEAM
ONE DAY EVENT
WISH FOR A PONY
CARGO OF HORSES
NO ENTRY
STOLEN PONIES
WE HUNTED HOUNDS
RIDERS FROM AFAR
HORSES AT HOME
I WANTED A PONY
RIDING WITH THE LYNTONS
JACKY JUMPS TO THE TOP
FIRST PONY
STABLE TO LET
PONIES ON THE HEATHER
THE SURPRISE RIDING CLUB

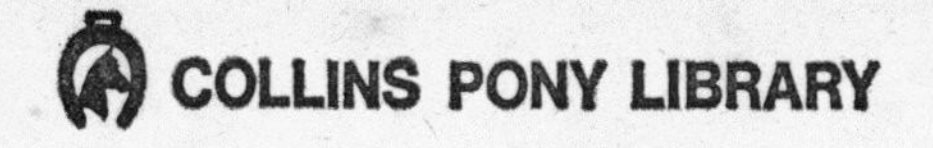

A PONY FOR TWO

Denise Hill

COLLINS
LONDON & GLASGOW

First printed in this new edition 1973

ISBN 0 00 164318 5

PRINTED AND MADE IN GREAT BRITAIN BY
WILLIAM COLLINS SONS AND CO. LTD.
LONDON AND GLASGOW

CONTENTS

". . . there used to be in the days of not so long ago what were called the 'whisperers'. These were horsemen who could gain the attention, and eventually the obedience, of any horse, however vicious, by whispering to it. What was whispered was a closely guarded secret and it is likely that the words were of little account, it being the tone that mattered. Such people could walk up to a strange horse in a field, approach it, stand still and whisper to the animal. After that the horse became the humble servant of the whisperer. This claim was ridiculed by some, but from personal experience I am convinced that certain people really possessed this curious gift."

From 'How Animals Talk' by
R. H. SMYTHE, M.R.C.V.S.
Country Life Ltd.

CHAPTER ONE

PLANS FOR A PONY

JEREMY FORTUNE and his sister Jane had been keen on horses ever since they could remember. "Mad on horses" their parents called it.

They spent every spare moment of the school holidays at the riding stables, cleaning tack, fetching and carrying, "mucking out" the stalls and loose-boxes. They could not afford to pay for rides very often, and Miss Long, who ran the stables, was not rich either. She could not give Jeremy and Jane unlimited free rides, but she recognised real enthusiasm when she saw it, and she helped as much as she could. During the slack season she gave them an occasional riding lesson, and they too saved up their pocket money for an occasional "real" ride, and were grateful for a chance of a trot down to the blacksmith's with a couple of horses.

The Fortunes lived near Lymington, in the New Forest. All their lives Jeremy and Jane had been familiar with the little half-wild New Forest ponies that lived care-free lives around them. They went every year to the auction sales at the Beaulieu Road Sale Yard and saw, rather sadly, the proud, unruly little ponies sold and taken away, their muddy coats covering their bulging grass-filled sides.

Miss Long had bought a couple once for her riding school and Jeremy and Jane had helped to break them to the saddle. But they had turned out to be obstinate, self-willed little things that needed firm handling. Jeremy and Jane could manage them, but they were not suitable for children just starting to ride, and Miss Long had sold them into private ownership.

But it was this experiment that first put the idea into Jane's head, and she brought it out one day as she and Jeremy were cleaning tack up at the stables.

"Wouldn't it be wonderful if we could have a pony of our own—half each!" she said wistfully.

"Don't be a goop!" Jeremy scoffed. "You know they cost an awful lot. Miss Long paid about forty pounds each for hers."

"I don't mean now, this minute," Jane explained. "But when we're a bit older. Supposing we saved up for—for two years or something like that?"

Jeremy finished off the bit he was polishing, and sat down on an upturned bucket to consider before he replied.

"Um . . . there's the money we spend on rides now . . . we could save that . . ."

"And our birthdays and Christmases—we could perhaps have money instead of presents——" Jane was hopping up and down with excitement.

"And Mr. Hutchinson—you know, at Brockenhurst Farm—I helped him with the evening milking last week and he said if I liked to come in the early morning during the holidays he'd give me a bit of pocket money for helping. He can't pay me real wages because I'm not old enough, but it'd be a bit to save up."

"Oh, Jeremy—that would be clever of you!" Then Jane's face fell. "But I must think of something to do too——"

"You can't expect to do much when you're only nine," said Jeremy loftily, then relented a little. "But it's an idea, all the same, about a pony. We'd have to find somewhere to keep it that wouldn't cost much . . ."

"We'd find somewhere—once we had the pony," said

Jane decisively. "Supposing we got a foal—about nine months old? They don't cost nearly so much."

"No-o," said Jeremy slowly. "I know they don't, but the trouble is you don't know how big they're going to grow at that age, and as I'll be about thirteen by the time we could ride it I'd probably be too big for it if it only turned out a twelve or thirteen hander. No, your first idea was best, Jane—to save up until we can afford to buy a two-or-three-year-old. Here, calm down! You nearly had the bucket over then! And anyway it's no good getting excited, because at the rate we'll be able to save up it'll be at least two years of no pocket money and no real rides!"

"I don't care! It'll be worth it, every time!" said Jane stoutly. "We'll have a proper campaign. And we won't tell anybody until we've got nearly enough saved up!"

And for the next two years they stuck to their campaign. Occasionally there was a bit of a set-back—like the time when their mother was in hospital and they took out two pounds from their savings and bought her a great big bunch of roses, in the middle of winter, because they were her favourite flowers.

But the little fund in the Post Office mounted steadily. Jeremy uncomplainingly got up at five o'clock all through the school holidays and helped with the morning milking at Brockenhurst Farm. And Jane did find some way of helping after all. She enjoyed knitting and was quite good at it, and she took in orders for dolls' clothes and even babies' knitted woollies.

But now that the price was not such a distant goal they had to face up to the great problem of keeping the pony once they had it.

"Yes, it is about time we started thinking about it," agreed Jane. They were sitting in the dining-room finishing their homework one day before Christmas. They had just counted up the contents of their Post Office accounts, and it had reached the comfortable little sum of £43.83½p. between them.

"You see, it's taken us nearly two years to save up that!" said Jeremy. "But there wouldn't be enough coming in to keep the pony. I mean, we'll have to rent a field, and have some sort of shelter in it—and we can't expect to work him much without some extra food besides grass. It wouldn't be fair." He got up and walked over to the window moodily. "Oh, dear, sometimes I just feel like giving up!"

Jane flung down her pencil and clenched her fists.

"I'm not going to give up!" she said fiercely. "Something will happen—I know. I'm going to *will* for a miracle!"

Jeremy was shocked.

"Jane! Miracles don't happen for ordinary things like us getting a pony—you mustn't talk like that!"

But Jane wasn't listening. She had her eyes tight shut and her face was screwed up with concentration.

Suddenly there was a sharp rat-tat on the front door, and she opened her eyes again resignedly.

"Bother! It's disturbed my willing!" she said crossly.

"Answer it, will you, Jeremy?" called his mother from the other room.

Jeremy was gone for some minutes and it wasn't until his mother called out: "Do shut that front door, dear. Bring whoever it is inside!"

"It's all right—it was only the paper." Jeremy took the evening paper into his parents and then came back slowly into the dining-room. Jane's eyes widened when she saw his face.

"You look funny!" she said. "What's happened?"

"You did will something, after all," answered Jeremy. "That was Bandy Rogers at the door."

Jane frowned.

"What's he got to do with horses?" she said. "He can't ride. It's just that his legs are naturally like that——"

"Shut up a minute and listen!" said Jeremy. "He's just told me something! He's giving up the evening paper round—and I'll be taking over for him! He's mentioned me to Mr. James at the shop and Mr. James said if I like to look in to-morrow, the job's mine! And it's one pound a week!"

"Golly!" breathed Jane. "D'you think that'd be enough to keep a pony?"

"I think so," said Jeremy. "It wouldn't cost much in the summer and we could save then for the winter when it would need more food."

Jane pushed her chair back and stood up.

"You know what—it's time we told Mummy and Daddy," she said decidedly. "Now it's getting so—so possible we must talk to them about it. Come on, I'm going in now!"

Jeremy looked at his sister. When she stuck out her chin like that he knew her mind was made up.

"All right, but don't go expecting them to leap at the idea," he warned her.

Mr. and Mrs. Fortune were sitting by the fire in the next room.

"Finished your homework?" said Mrs. Fortune, smiling up at them. "Did you remember to turn off the fire?"

"I did it," said Jane. She took a deep breath and jumped right in to her story with both feet. "Daddy, Mummy! Jeremy and I want to buy a pony. We've been saving up for ages, but we didn't want to tell anyone until we'd got a good bit behind us. And we have—we've got over forty pounds now, and there's Christmas and our birthdays to come yet, and we were hoping that by next August we should have enough to go down to the Beaulieu Road Sale and get a two- or three-year-old, probably a three-year-old if we can afford it——" she paused for lack of breath.

Their father's eyebrows had climbed so far up his forehead as Jane went on that they had almost disappeared into his hair. But he didn't laugh, and he spoke gently and firmly.

"So that's what you've both been saving up for!" he said. "We knew there was something in the wind with all this business of money instead of presents. But a pony . . . you ought to know, both of you, that buying it is less than half the problem. It costs a good deal to keep a horse when you've got to rent the land to keep it on. Much more than you could afford, even saving all you can."

"But now there's Ba . . ." Jane started.

Jeremey gave his sister a look that said "Shut up!" and turned to his father.

"Don't listen to Jane—she will rush things!" he said. "We didn't tell you about it before, because it was the question of keeping it that bothered us too. But to-night something happened——"

"It was Bandy Rogers—he came along like a—a miracle!" the irrepressible Jane burst in.

"He's giving up the evening paper round because he starts work next week," explained Jeremy. "And Mr. James has said I can have the job if I want it. Can I Dad, since I want to?"

"I don't see why not," said his father. "And you reckon that would pay for the keep of the pony?"

"Just about—less in the summer and more in the winter," explained Jeremy.

"So if we save up a bit more, and if we can find somewhere to keep it, and if we can earn enough money to look after it properly—would you mind us having a pony?" Jane brought out all in one breath.

Mr. and Mrs. Fortune met each others' eyes and suddenly laughed.

"All those if's—and one more," said their father. "*If* it doesn't interfere with your school work, well, then, I suppose we can say we don't object, can't we dear?" he addressed his wife. Then he turned back to Jeremy, and his face was serious. "It's a pretty big thing to take on. Can you do it?"

"I know we can!" said Jeremy stoutly.

But later on, as he lay in bed, he didn't feel quite so sure. Perhaps it *was* a lot to take on. A pony took a lot of feeding, and a lot of looking after.

There was a sudden spatter of rain against the windows, and Jeremy thought gloomily that it would need a shelter in the winter, too.

Just then he heard a faint click, and the door opened.

"Jeremy, are you still awake?" It was Jane's whisper.

"Yes, but what on earth are you doing?"

"I've thought of something." She came in and climbed on to his bed, where she sat hugging her toes. "It was the rain made me think of it. You see, it makes the ground wet . . . " she paused.

"I hope you haven't come in just to tell me something I know already," said Jeremy scathingly.

"No, really I haven't. It's the rain—it made me think of water and then I thought of the water meadow. You know, the one down the lane, with that old broken-down shed in the corner. Couldn't it be patched up?"

Jeremy sat straight up in bed.

"It—it *is* an idea!" he said. "We'd have to ask, of course. I don't know who owns it——"

"Well, you ought to," said Jane rather smugly. "It's Mr. Hutchinson who you did the milking for last holidays! Lindy Hutchinson told me. She's in my class and we were talking about it because there are water buttercups there in the spring and we're doing them in nature——"

"All right—pipe down!" said Jeremy. He began to feel that Jane was taking charge a bit too much. "Anyway, if we do get permission, it'd have to be me to do the shed. Girls can't do carpentering."

Jane wasn't really listening.

"Let's go along and ask him before school in the morning," she said. "I know it's quite a long time yet before we get our pony, but it would be nice to get something settled!" She yawned. "Well, I'd better get back to bed because we must get up early!"

The next morning their mother greeted them with some surprise as they appeared for breakfast an hour earlier than usual.

"We've got something we must do before school," Jeremy explained.

"Something about the horse. We'll tell you afterwards," added Jane.

Mrs. Fortune shot them a quick glance, but she didn't say any more.

"Let's have a look at the water meadow first," said Jane, pulling on her wellington boots in the porch.

They walked down the lane and climbed over the gate into the water meadow. In many ways it was a good place to keep a horse, especially in dry weather. The disadvantage was that it was almost under water in the winter. A small stream formed the boundary of one side, and in wet weather it overflowed its banks. Over to one side was a slightly raised piece of ground with a building that had once been a shed, but was now derelict with a tattered and broken roof.

"It's pretty wet," said Jeremy after they had stared glumly for a while. "I know New Forest ponies are used to boggy land, but this is practically a lake."

"It'd mean the grass would be super when there's a drought everywhere else," put in Jane optimistically. "And there's the shed. We could keep him up if it really got too wet."

"Um. Let's have a look at the shed, then."

"Oh, J.—it doesn't look much good!" said Jane disappointedly.

"I dunno. I think I might be able to do something with it," said Jeremy, measuring up with his eye. "After all, we don't want anything elaborate, just something moderately weather proof. I reckon I could do it up all right."

Jane shot him a glance of admiration, which he pretended not to see.

"Anyway," he went on. "We haven't got it yet! We'd better hurry and get over to Mr. Hutchinson's."

Mr. Hutchinson had been in some time from his milking and was just finishing his breakfast. His daughter Lindy greeted Jane and tried to drag her off, but Jane shook her head.

"I can't play now, Lindy. We've got some business to do with your father," she said importantly.

Mrs. Hutchinson stared at the two children for a moment, then smiled.

"Business, eh? Come on, Lindy, we'll leave them to it," she said cheerfully, giving the reluctant Lindy a tray of breakfast things to carry out as she followed her.

Mr. Hutchinson sat down by the fire and motioned the two children to sit down too. "Well, let's hear it," he said, taking out his pipe.

Jeremy saw Jane opening her mouth, and hastened to get his word in first.

"It's not exactly real business," he said. "It's just a sort of question. You know your water meadow at the bottom of our lane, Mr. Hutchinson? Well, Jane and I wondered

—that is—if we ever have a pony of our own—because we might do one day——" Jeremy floundered a little, then went on: "What we meant was, would you let us keep him there, and how much would it cost?"

"And the shed, Jeremy, don't forget the shed!" whispered Jane.

"Oh, yes, if we can keep a pony there, would you let me mend up the shed for a shelter in the winter?"

Jeremy stopped, and there was silence for a moment. Then Mr. Hutchinson blew a great cloud of smoke from his pipe.

"There's a lot of if's about this deal," he said slowly.

"That's what Daddy said!" Jane put in. "But there aren't really. We've sorted out most of the if's, and yours is about the last one."

He seemed to understand, for he nodded.

"I can say this," he told them. "That water meadow's good grazing in the summer, but it's too wet for crops. It'd mean keeping your pony up a good deal if we have a really wet spell, otherwise he'd get foot rot. I haven't got any particular use in mind for it at the moment—nor for the old shed. I reckon I can say yes. When would you be wanting it?"

"Not for a while yet—probably next September or thereabouts," Jeremy told him. "Thanks, though. It's very good of you, Mr. Hutchinson. And how much would the rent be, d'you think, please?"

"We-ell," Mr. Hutchinson gave a glance at their eager faces. "I don't reckon you'd want to pay much, what with having to buy fodder in the winter . . ."

"No—we couldn't afford an awful lot," said Jeremy honestly.

Mr. Hutchinson puffed out more clouds of smoke from his pipe before he spoke again.

"Let's put it like this," he said finally. "You agree to buy your fodder from me. I'll let you have it just over cost price. It'll be less than you'd pay at the corn merchants. I reckon that'll pay me for the use of the water meadow. Now, just a moment." He pulled a piece of paper towards him. "This here's the current price of hay and oats, and here's the price you'd pay me. Straw I can let you have; I'd get the value back in manure when the pony's kept up at nights."

Jeremy looked at the figures and went bright red. He knew the prices of food from Miss Long, and he realised that on those figures the farmer was making practically nothing on the deal.

"That—that's awfully good of you——" he stammered. "But it's nearly free——"

"I like to see a bit of enterprise in youngsters," grunted the farmer. "When did you say you expect to get your pony?"

"We might have enough by the August sale at Beaulieu Road," Jeremy told him. "We want an unbroken two or three year old, if there is one going at our price."

"That's the best way—to break it in yourselves," nodded the farmer. He rose to his feet and stretched. "Beaulieu Road—I go up there for most of the sales. Let me know and I'll maybe be able to bring the horse back for you in my box."

Jeremy and Jane fairly danced out of the farmhouse.

"Isn't he a darling!" said Jane. "Oh J., I just feel it's going to be all right—everything's going so beautifully!"

"It's gone smoothly so far," said Jeremy repressively. "But there's plenty of time for things to go wrong yet!"

CHAPTER TWO

THE BIRTHDAY

BUT IT didn't seem that Jeremy's gloomy prophecy was to be fulfilled, for things continued to go smoothly, though their savings did not mount up very fast, because Jeremy spent the first few weeks' paper-round money on materials for repairing the old shed in the water meadow. His father helped him with the heavy work, and Mr. Hutchinson turned up trumps again with some good timber to make a proper stable-type door. Before long they had a rough-looking but reasonably serviceable loose-box.

"It's not exactly a palace," said Jeremy doubtfully, stepping back to survey his handiwork.

"I think it's beautiful," said Jane loyally. "I'd love to live there if I were a horse."

She was sitting on a log outside the shed, watching Jeremy and his father working. She was wrapped up against the chilly spring breeze, but her hands were bare—they had to be because she was knitting busily. In fact, every spare moment she had was filled, because there had been a spate of orders through Mrs. Hutchinson and the Mothers' Union, and Jane took her knitting with her wherever she went.

"Coo-ee!" came a voice from the gate, and they saw their mother coming across the meadow waving a letter.

"Mummy, you look awfully pleased," said Jane. "What's happened? Who's the letter from?"

"A surprise," smiled her mother. "It's from Uncle Leslie. He's coming down to stay for a while!"

"Wow!" Jeremy's head appeared out of the top half of the shed door. "That's smashing! When's he coming?"

Mrs. Fortune looked at the letter in her hand.

"He doesn't say exactly," she admitted. "But he says: 'I'll be in time for the Birthday!' "

Jane's birthday was the same day as Jeremy's, though she had been born two years later, so they always had a joint celebration.

"Oh, lovely!" she said. "We can tell him all about our horse! And he'll be able to help us break it in, if we want any help. He knows such an awful lot about horses because of living with Arabs—I mean the people, but they had horses as well."

"How long can he stay?" Jeremy interrupted. Jane did tend to run on rather.

"He says he's got 'indefinite leave'," said their mother. "But you know how it is—things happen to Leslie!"

Jeremy grinned appreciatively. He certainly knew how it was. Uncle Leslie was their mother's brother, and his job was something connected with Interpol. The children didn't know the full details, but their uncle was liable to be away for months at a time and then suddenly turn up in England looking bronzed and a little haggard. There wasn't any part of the world that Uncle Leslie hadn't been in at some time, and wherever he was he managed to find horses.

Mr. Fortune, hearing his wife's voice, came round from behind the shed where he had been strengthening the supports.

"Hallo, dear. Tea time?" he said hopefully.

"Really, you're as bad as the children!" she laughed. "I came to tell you about this letter from Leslie. But you come back with me, and the children can follow in about ten minutes when they've tidied up here."

Jane put away her knitting and gave Jeremy a hand with collecting the tools together after her parents had gone.

"Isn't it lovely about Uncle Leslie! I think he's the most grand person to have as an uncle," she said.

"Yes," agreed Jeremy. "It's funny, though. When you think of all the brave things he's done you imagine a great hefty chap, but Uncle Leslie's quite small for a man, really."

"He's stronger than most people, anyway," said Jane. "D'you remember those sacks he picked up and flung into the lorry when that delivery man was making a fuss about it? They weighed two tons or something."

"Two hundredweight, you nitwit!" Jeremy squashed her. "Two tons is more what the lorry weighed!"

"Well, all the same——" Jane wasn't to be outdone. "All the same, I'm glad Uncle Leslie isn't big and fat, because he'll be able to ride our pony!"

"Talking about that——" Jeremy said. "We must go over our Post Office books and see how things are going. I've had to spend a bit on this shed."

"I've already been over them," said Jane. "It hasn't grown very much lately. We'll have to be pretty lucky on our birthday to go to the August sales."

Jeremy gave the smallest of sighs. For the last two Christmases and birthdays they had stuck to their resolve and had chosen money instead of presents when given the choice. They had had all the fun of giving their own presents to Mum and Dad at Christmas, of course, but there was no use pretending that the pile of envelopes waiting to be opened was as much fun as a heap of large crackly parcels.

They heard no more from their Uncle Leslie for the next week, but they didn't worry. If Uncle Leslie said he would be there for their birthday they knew he would. So when they came downstairs on their birthday morning Jeremy looked at Jane's rather solemn face and nudged her.

"We did ask for money instead," he said. "Come on, look happy, Janey! And don't forget Uncle Leslie's coming!"

"He rang up late last night." Their mother had heard this last remark. "He'll be here some time this morning." She kissed Jane and rumpled Jeremy's hair. "Happy birthday, both of you!"

When they came to open the envelopes they found one that they didn't expect. It was rather grimy, and inside was a scrap of paper torn off a brown paper bag. In large straggly capitals on it was written:

"ONE SET OF SHOES FOR FORTUNES' PONY. FREE." And it was signed: "JOS. MARLOW."

"Old Joe—the blacksmith!" cried Jane. "But how did he . . . oh, I suppose it was through the Hutchinsons."

"I think most people in the village know," said their mother. "There seem to be a few parcels, anyway."

There was a neat, long-shaped parcel from Miss Long at the riding school. Inside was a really lovely little snaffle bridle, the leather supple and well-cared for.

"This was the bridle I had for my own pony when I was young," the note said. "With thanks for all the help you have given me."

"Gosh!" said Jeremy in awe. "That *is* decent of her, because she's given us rides and lessons for the work we did and anyway we enjoyed it."

"Look, there's another parcel," said their mother. "Linda Hutchinson brought it over yesterday, and I had to keep it hidden."

The children undid the odd-shaped rather lumpy parcel and were delighted to find a set of grooming tools—body brush, dandy brush and curry comb.

"Aren't people *kind*! I do think we're lucky!" cried Jane,

and even Jeremy was beaming all over his face, forgetting to be pessimistic for once.

"Who's lucky?" said a voice at that moment, and a familiar figure walked into the room. In all the excitement and the rustling of paper they hadn't heard him open the back door.

"Uncle Leslie!" and "Leslie!" the children and their mother cried out together. Jeremy and Jane flung themselves on him.

"I hope you're here for a long time——"

"Because we're going to have a pony——"

"And you'll be able to help us ride him——"

"You'll come to the auction too, won't you——"

"Here—steady on!" laughed their uncle. "One thing at a time. Yes, I do know about your pony, because your mother told me when I rang up last night. I rather wormed it out of her, because I wanted to know something you would like for your birthday and it was lucky because I've brought something back with me that'll do rather well. Would you like to bring it in. It's in the boot of my car."

The children made a concerted rush for the door, though they did remember to say in advance "Thank you!" After a few minutes they came staggering back with a sizeable wooden crate carried between them.

Their father produced tools and they got it open, and carefully lifted out the contents from a nest of shavings. As it came into view the children gasped, for it was the loveliest saddle they had ever seen. The leather was shining with cleanliness, the stirrups were of chased silver, and the whole thing was light yet beautifully strong and well-made.

"It's wonderful!" breathed Jane.

"Uncle Leslie, where did you get such a beautiful saddle? I've never seen one like it in my life. Look at the workmanship on the stirrups alone!" There was awe in Jeremy's voice.

"It's a long story. But it was given to me by an old friend, one of the greatest horsemen I've ever known. He left it to me when he lay dying." Uncle Leslie paused, and said soberly. "It was a great honour, because it was the saddle belonging to his favourite Arab pony. It should fit any horse up to fourteen and a half hands, because it's well designed and shaped. And I know you'll take care of it."

"You bet we will!" said Jeremy solemnly. "Thank you Uncle Leslie. We feel honoured too."

"I didn't think we'd have anything so perfect as this," declared Jane.

"Well, that's all right, then. Many happy returns of the day!" said Uncle Leslie, rather belatedly.

It was a splendid birthday after all. They had a wonderful dinner with sausages and chips—Jeremy's favourite—and ice cream with pineapple—Jane's choice—for pudding.

"I like turkey too," Jeremy explained. "But that seems much more a Christmasy thing. Where were you at Christmas, Uncle Leslie?"

"Let me see now—Christmas . . ." Uncle Leslie considered. "Oh, yes, I was with an Arab tribe. There were eight of us in the family I was with—that's counting the horses."

"Were the horses in with you?" said Jane, round-eyed.

"Rather! The Arabs regard their horses as people," said Uncle Leslie. "In fact they look after them better than they look after themselves."

"I shall, too, when we have our pony," decided Jane.

Jeremy changed the subject hurriedly before Jane could announce that she was going to have the horse to sleep in her bedroom or something daft like that.

"Come for a walk this afternoon, Uncle Leslie," he said.

"We can go along the Heath Road and we'll probably see some ponies. There are some still out."

After dinner they put on their mackintoshes and stepped out into the slight drizzle. It had cleared by the time they reached the Heath Road—so called because the New Forest just here was open land, gorse and heather-covered later on, though just now it was dull and wintry-looking.

"Look, there are some ponies!" It was Jane's sharp eyes that spotted the moving dots in the distance.

Uncle Leslie shaded his eyes with his hand.

"Yes, I make it seven of them. They look more like brown bears with their winter coats." He stopped and screwed up his eyes to see better. "Just a minute, one of them's a bit different, though——"

The children followed the direction of his finger, and Jeremy said:

"Yes, that's a grey. It's a mare—we've seen her about with the others before, but only in the distance. She won't come up to be fed, even when the others do. Of course no one's supposed to feed them, but most of them make a bit of a nuisance of themselves with picnickers."

"Uncle Leslie," said Jane. "Every time I see that grey pony I seem to remember something. I don't know if it's a dream or not. Something about a lot of people and a man riding a grey horse that was sort of dancing——"

Uncle Leslie was staring at her with amazement.

"That's not a dream, Jane. It was a circus we took you to. But you were only three. I shouldn't have thought you'd remember it."

"I remember it too—but I couldn't go! It was when I was getting over chicken-pox, and I know I was jolly upset!" cried Jeremy.

"I don't remember any of the circus except the horse," Jane admitted. "Did the man riding it wear a top hat and make a sort of noise like this to his horse——" she gave a kind of chirruping whistle.

"That's the noise she always makes to horses," Jeremy put in. He stopped as he caught sight of uncle's face. "Uncle Leslie, what're you thinking about? You look awfully odd!"

"It was just that Jane reminded me of something," said Uncle Leslie slowly.

"Tell us!" demanded Jane. "It sounds like a story!"

"It is, in a way," said Uncle Leslie. "It's bound up with the saddle I gave you."

"I knew there was a story about that!" said Jane with satisfaction.

"Have you heard of *haute école*—high school-riding?" asked their uncle.

"Oh, yes, it's a kind of very special riding," said Jeremy. "Things like cantering on the spot, and piaffes and pirouettes——"

"Pirouettes are dancing!" Jane put in. "What I saw that horse doing at the circus!"

"Well, *haute école* isn't really a circus thing," said Uncle Leslie. "The Spanish *haute école* is a highly skilled art, and there is a school for it in Vienna. But there was a family I knew in Spain who had carried on the tradition of Spanish *haute école* for generations. As you know, I've done a bit of riding myself, and by good luck I was able to do a good turn to one of the young grandsons—found him with a broken leg and took him home. They were an amazing family, and I was very fortunate to be accepted as a friend. The grandfather, Emilio Toral, was at that time the head of the family. He did not ride much himself but he kept an iron hand on the rest of the family. His sons travelled all over the world, giving exhibitions of Spanish *haute école* with the grey Arab horses which they bred themselves.

One of the sons came to England with his Arab stallion. But Ramiro was a wild, extravagant sort of chap, and he got badly into debt. He did not dare to tell his father and, when he got an offer of good pay for making his horse 'dance' in a circus he accepted. It would have broken his father's heart to know how the art of *haute école* was being debased—but how the public loved Ramiro and Brioso, his dancing horse! It was he whom Jane saw that time. But soon after that I had to go to Egypt for some years, and I rather lost touch with the Toral family. In fact I only saw old Emilio once more, when he was dying. I was in Madrid for a couple of days and met one of the granddaughters of the family, who was now married. She told me the old man was very ill and had been asking for me, and I went out for a hurried visit. He was very weak. He just rallied enough to tell me he wanted me to have the saddle, 'for someone who will truly value it,' was what he said. He seemed glad to see me again, though."

"And what happened to—Ramiro, was it?—who was over here performing in circuses?" asked Jeremy, absorbed.

"I didn't hear any more of him," admitted Uncle Leslie. "But knowing him I suspect that he didn't leave circus work once he had started it. As a guest artist he could make really big money, especially abroad—as long as he kept up his standard. His father always considered him rather a bad hat—not as far as horses were concerned, of course, because no Toral could ever ill-treat a horse. But the old man thought Ramiro debased the pure Spanish *haute école* technique and made it showy and—well, circusy, to invent a word."

He paused and looked over at the group of horses, which were moving into the shelter of the trees now.

"I wish you could have seen those Arabs which the Toral family bred," he said. "They were beautiful, with the most perfect heads and a lovely free movement. Funnily enough, just for a moment that grey put me in mind of them—the same kind of stride."

"But she's only a New Forest pony," said Jane.

"I suppose she is," said Uncle Leslie. "But look, now she's trotting. There's some breeding there I should think. I wonder who her owner is—or are they just wild?"

"Oh, no, they all belong to owners who have rights of common grazing," explained Jeremy. "But they let them run wild and breed in the Forest."

He looked again at the group of ponies. Now that his uncle mentioned it Jeremy could see that the grey had an attractive, lithe action. But it was really too far off to see properly.

"Perhaps she'll turn up at the August sales," he said. "Then we can get a closer look at her."

It had started to rain again now, and they turned for home. Suddenly Jeremy's last remark registered with Jane, who turned a wet, shining face to her brother.

"So you do think we'll have enough money to go to the August auction!" she said.

"Don't get too excited about it," said Jeremy repressively. "With the paper-round money we should be able to have a look round, anyway, but the prices may be too high for us."

Jane wasn't listening—she was dancing up and down.

"I do hope the grey's there!" she said. "She must be rising three by now—just the age we want. I'd love to have her, wouldn't you, J.? She's much the nicest pony I've seen."

"You definitely want an unbroken pony?" asked Uncle Leslie.

"Oh, yes, it'll be much more our very own. Half Jeremy's and half mine, you see."

"Well, don't quarrel about whose half is which!" grinned their uncle. "Neither of you would get far on half a horse!"

Jane giggled, and said: "Don't worry, Uncle Leslie, we won't quarrel. Jeremy's paying more than I am, but I'll have to do more of the looking after in school time, because I get home earlier, and he's not home till after dark in the winter."

"You'll come to the auction, won't you?" Jeremy asked his uncle.

"You bet I'll be there!" he smiled. "If I have to go away I'll leave you my address so you can let me know the date."

That night Jane couldn't sleep. She crept into Jeremy's room and found him awake too.

"I can't believe it's really getting near!" she sighed. "Our own pony . . ."

She padded over to the window. There was quiet, cold silver moonlight over everything, and away in the distance, silhouetted on the horizon, she could see the proud figure of a solitary horse.

"It's one of the stallions," declared Jeremy.

Jane suddenly shivered.

"He gives me a feeling," was all she would say.

"It's no slippers on that's making you shiver," said Jeremy. Jane did sometimes get "feelings", and there was usually some reason for it, but it didn't do to encourage her to be fanciful.

But all the same, after she had gone back to bed, he looked for rather a long time at the noble, lonely figure of the horse on the skyline.

CHAPTER THREE

FALLA

THE ANNUAL auction sales at the Beaulieu Road Sale Yard were held at the end of August, the end of September, and the end of October. After much consultation, and a period of going round with their lips moving as they did arithmetic in their heads, Jeremy and Jane decided to wait until the October sales.

"There's not such a crowd for those," Jeremy told his parents. "We've got a better chance of picking up a good pony at a reasonable price."

He and Jane went down to the August and September sales to see how the prices were going. They found that the average price of a fourteen hand three-year-old was in the region of sixty pounds. That was the sum that they hoped to have by October, so they felt reasonably hopeful.

Neither of them spoke about the grey mare that they had seen when Uncle Leslie was with them. But each knew what the other was thinking. The grey was not up for sale at either of the first two auctions, and when Jane heaved a sigh of relief after the second one Jeremy knew what it was for.

"Don't set your mind on—any particular kind of horse, Janey," he said. Somehow he felt it would be unlucky to mention the actual one.

"I'm trying not to," said Jane. "But I keep on having a feeling about it, all the same."

Their Uncle Leslie was away visiting friends, but they

wrote to him and told him the date of the sale, and a reply came on a postcard: "Hope to make it—meet you there. Leslie."

Mr. Hutchinson had told them that he would meet them at the sale, and had promised to bring back their pony if they bought one. They hurried through their breakfast and their morning chores and caught the bus down to the Sale Yard.

Jane sniffed appreciatively.

"Lovely smell of horses!" she said.

The New Forest ponies were in small fenced corrals in groups of five or six of the same age, with an occasional single one or couple in a smaller enclosure. Over the far side were the horse lines where those horses and ponies which had been broken or partly broken were tethered by halters.

Jeremy did not spare more than a glance for the foals; Jane would have liked to spend more time with the little things, but he kept her strictly to business.

"I know they're nice, but don't forget we want to ride, not have a pet lamb!" he said firmly. "Come on, let's look at the two and three year olds."

They made their way over to the pens holding the older ponies, and suddenly Jane clutched Jeremy's arm.

"She's there! I knew she would be! I told you I had a feeling about it!" she cried, pointing to one of the small pens.

Sure enough, Jeremy could recognise the grey mare that they had seen on the heathland. She was by herself in a small pen and she was moving her feet and tossing her head nervously, her large dark eyes full of alarm.

Jeremy whistled. "Phew! She's a beauty all right. Look at that head!"

Even the mare's rough and muddy condition could not

disguise the breeding that showed in her small head and short back and strong, arched neck.

"She's awfully scared, poor dear." Jane sounded almost in tears.

The children approached the fence, and Jeremy held out his hand, speaking quietly to the mare. But she backed farther into the corner, her nostrils flaring, her small, intelligent ears pricked.

"She's not bad-tempered," said Jane. "Look, her ears are forward, not back. She's only feeling strange and worried. I'm going into her."

"Jane, come back! You'll frighten her worse than ever!" cried Jeremy, but it was too late. Jane was inside the pen, and was walking fearlessly up to the grey pony.

"The silly kid!" whispered Jeremy. "She'll . . . oh, help!"

For as Jane approached the mare backed still more, and feeling her quarters touch the fence behind her, knew she could not retreat farther. The next moment she had reared high in the air, with Jane, looking very small, just under those sharp hooves!

Jeremy opened his mouth to shout, but no sound came. He was too far off to do anything, and no one seemed to have noticed Jane—it had all happened so quickly.

With a gasp he pulled himself together and made for the fence, but as he reached it he stopped and stared in amazement.

For Jane had everything under control. She had taken one step backwards to give the mare room to come down, and had her hand held out, as she made that odd little chirrup she always used to horses. And the grey mare had dropped her forefeet to the ground and was standing still too, her ears pricked forward and her eyes fixed on Jane.

Jane didn't move, and slowly the grey stretched her head

forward and sniffed at Jane's outstretched hand. Still chirruping, Jane moved her hand towards herself, and the grey pony took a hesitant step forward. Slowly Jane slid her hand up and stroked the pony's neck, talking to her now in a low voice. Her other hand was feeling in her pocket and she pulled out a rather fluffy piece of carrot. The grey smelt it, blew gently down her nostrils, and accepted it.

Jane, never ceasing to talk quietly, reached up her hand and took hold of the pony's forelock. To Jeremy's astonishment the grey followed her as she led her back to the fence, and though she tried to check when she saw Jeremy standing there, she advanced once more when Jane spoke to her.

"It's all right—you can stroke her now, J.," said Jane. "It was only that she isn't very used to people yet."

In a kind of daze Jeremy put up his hand and stroked the grey's neck. "Mind she doesn't rear again," he said.

"She won't—she's promised," said Jane confidently. "Look at her lovely head—have you ever seen such an intelligent look in a horse's eye?"

Jeremy stepped back and studied the grey carefully. Her shape left something to be desired—after a summer at grass her sides bulged like balloons. But her shoulders and quarters were strong, and she had a good depth of girth. At the moment she had relaxed under Jane's caressing hand, and was standing on three legs and the tip of one hind foot, looking slumped and elderly. But suddenly something caught her attention, and her head came up, nostrils flaring and ears alert.

"See?" said Jane.

"Yes," said Jeremy thoughtfully. "She's got a really thoroughbred look, all right. Let's have a look at the catalogue."

"There's 'FD' branded on her back," said Jane.

"Yes, here we are: Grey mare, 14 hands, rising three years: dam, Betsy Jane (N.F.)."

"Same name as me!" breathed Jane.

"Sire unknown . . . owner, J. Fildred of Winchester." Jeremy looked again at the grey. "We'll try for her all right, but I hope her price doesn't go too high."

A sudden commotion behind them made him turn his head.

"Look, the auctioneer's coming in now!" he said. "Come on, we must get near him, or he won't see us bidding!"

The two children wriggled their way through the crowd which had collected round the fenced ring in front of the auctioneer's rostrum. There was a passage, also fenced, which led into the ring, and the ponies were driven down this passage one by one. When they were in the ring those on the edge urged them on to move round to show off their action. The scene was incredibly noisy, and Jane couldn't help feeling sorry for the little ponies driven hither and thither, their eyes rolling wildly.

"Keep a look out for Uncle Leslie," said Jeremy in Jane's ear. "He said he'd be here. Bother this crowd—I can't see a thing."

"He'll find us," said Jane confidently. "I expect he's at the back somewhere."

The bidding was going on briskly now. The very young New Forest foals were going for prices between fifteen and twenty guineas each, but once they reached the two-year-olds the prices began to rise. Jeremy found that the average price was round about forty guineas, and he began to feel a little hopeful.

At last came the turn of the grey mare. She came snorting into the ring, her hooves hardly seeming to touch the ground. Then she halted, turning her beautiful head from side to side in a hunted kind of way.

"Now, ladies and gentlemen, I don't need to tell you that there's quality here!" shouted the auctioneer when he had gabbled through the particulars. "Gentle disposition too—make a good riding pony. Wake her up, Bill, let the ladies and gentlemen see her action!"

His assistant climbed into the ring, waving his arms and shouting at the grey. She did not move, so one of the bystanders handed him a whip, and he flicked her on the hind quarters.

The mare took objection to this. She wheeled, and the next moment had reared into the air, her forefeet lashing out and her nostrils flaring. Bill backed hurriedly away and tumbled out of the ring with undignified haste. The mare dropped to the ground again and stood with her ears back and tail lashing.

"'Er's a rearer," said a voice behind Jeremy. "'Er won't be no good for a kid's ride."

Jane flushed and was just about to turn and make an indignant reply when Jeremy squeezed her arm.

"Shut up!" he whispered. "Don't you see—it'll keep her price down if they think she rears!"

"She won't rear with us—I know it!" Jane whispered back, having the sense to keep her voice too low for anyone except Jeremy to hear.

The auctioneer had changed his tune a bit after the grey mare's exhibition of spirit.

"A fine, high-spirited mare, as you see, ladies and gentlemen," he cried. "Now who'll start me at thirty guineas for her? Come, gentlemen—a lovely little mare like this—your bids, please!"

"Lovely little circus 'orse!" said a voice from the back, and there was a wave of laughter, but no one took up the bidding at thirty guineas.

Finally a voice at the back said: "Fifteen."

The auctioneer looked pained.

"Of course I can see you're joking, sir," he said. "But will someone say twenty—a ridiculous bid—twenty guineas, thank you, sir . . . and five . . . and five more . . . y'see, there we are at thirty guineas where I wanted to start! Why waste my time?"

There was an appreciative guffaw from the crowd, and the bidding began to move more briskly. Thirty-five, forty, forty-five. Then there was a pause.

"Come, ladies and gentlemen—a finely bred mare like this . . . will someone say fifty . . . forty-six then . . .?"

Jeremy cleared his throat and opened his mouth, but his voice came out rather small, and it was Jane who called out loudly: "My brother says forty-six!"

"Forty-six I'm bid——" the auctioneer searched for the voice, spotted Jane waving her catalogue, and stopped, his eyebrows going up. "Are you a genuine bidder, young lady?"

"I'm the one!" called Jeremy, finding his voice. "Honestly, look!"

He pulled his Post Office book out of his inside pocket and showed it bulging with notes. The autioneer's eyes widened, and he bent over to speak quietly to Jeremy.

"You'd better let me look after that for you, sonny, just for the moment. Now it's been shown round, I wouldn't like it to be pinched."

Jeremy handed over the money without hesitation. He knew the auctioneer well from having seen him at the sales, and he had, truth to tell, been a little worried with all that money in his pocket.

The auctioneer straightened and went on with his business.

"I apologise for the interruption, ladies and gentlemen. Forty-six I'm bid by the young gentleman—seven over there—eight from the young gent—nine, thank you, sir!"

Jeremy's face had gone rather white. He had fifty pounds with him, and he knew that he would be able to borrow another two or three on his paper-round money. Fifty guineas was fifty-two pounds fifty pence—and his limit.

"Forty-nine guineas I'm bid—going once at forty-nine." The auctioneer was looking inquiringly at Jeremy, who found that his voice had disappeared again as it often did in moments of stress. But he raised his catalogue, and the auctioneer nodded.

"Fifty guineas from the young gentleman. Come, now, the mare's a bargain at that price! Going at fifty guineas . . ."

Jeremy put an arm round Jane, whether to support her or himself he didn't know. The auctioneer was raising his hammer and Jeremy held Jane so tightly he heard her give a little squeak. Then his heart gave a lurch and seemed to sink right into his boots. For the auctioneer was glancing towards the other side of the ring, where Jeremy could see two small dark men who hadn't bid so far. One of them raised his catalogue, and the auctioneer nodded, and went on smoothly:

". . . and one, thank you, sir—and two over on the left there . . . three . . . four . . . five . . . and six . . ." There was a pause and he glanced down at Jeremy. "And one more from you, young sir?"

Jeremy shook his head dumbly. He could see the small dark man over the other side glance beside him at his friend, who seemed to be counting money in a wallet, before he raised his catalogue once more.

"Fifty-seven guineas . . . any advance on fifty-seven?" The auctioneer glanced inquiringly round, but there was silence. He raised his hammer once more.

"Fifty-eight!" came a breathless voice from the back.

There was a murmur from the crowd and people craned

their necks to see who was bidding. Jeremy could see the two little dark men holding a rapid consultation, almost an argument, before one of them raised his catalogue again.

"Sixty!" came the inexorable voice from the back of the crowd, and this time the two dark men shrugged and shook their heads when the auctioneer glanced at them.

"Going once at sixty guineas—twice——" the auctioneer banged his hammer down. "Give your name and address to my clerk, would you please, sir." He addressed the bidder at the back of the crowd, then bent down to Jeremy. "Are you bidding for another pony, son?"

Jane had slipped away like a shadow from Jeremy's side, and on the point of following her he turned a distracted face to the auctioneer.

"Yes—no—I don't know yet. Please would you hold on to the money for the moment? I must go after my sister!"

"All right—it'll be safe with me," promised the auctioneer. "Better luck next time, eh, sonny?"

Jeremy weaved through the crowd in pursuit of Jane. He caught up with her on the outskirts and put his arm round her shoulders.

"I know it's rotten—I feel awful too," he said. "D'you want to come back and bid for another pony?"

"No! I don't want any other except that one." Jane pulled herself free. "Go away, Jeremy!"

Jeremy stood back as Jane ran blindly across the grass, and suddenly Jeremy saw a figure step into her path and field her neatly.

"Uncle Leslie!" she gasped.

"Now come along—that's not the way to behave!" said their uncle, giving Jane a little shake. "Hello, Jeremy—sorry I couldn't get here earlier. We nearly lost it, didn't we?"

"Lost w-what?" Jeremy felt a bit dazed.

"The grey, of course. As soon as I saw her I knew she was the only pony worthy of our attention. Luckily she played up a bit, which kept the price nearer what I wanted to pay. Because you've got a bargain there. I happened to spot our dark friends counting up their cash, so I thought I'd pip them at the post."

Jane was staring at him with a tear still wandering down one cheek.

"Uncle—d'you mean *you've bought the grey for us*?"

"Who else would I buy it for?" said her uncle, pulling one of her plaits.

"It's more than we've saved up——" Jeremy began.

"And the balance is a present from me," said Uncle Leslie decidedly. "Now—not another word. Come along and see her."

The grey mare was back in her pen, and the auctioneer's clerk greeted Uncle Leslie.

"You've bought the grey mare, sir?" he said. "Someone wanted to speak to you——" he looked round. "They seem to have gone for the moment, though."

"The auctioneer's still got my money," Jeremy told his uncle, who nodded.

"That's all right—I'll make out a cheque and get it back when he's finished the deal he's on now," he said.

Jeremy left the business side to his uncle and joined Jane who was talking to the grey.

"She's as gentle as gentle," Jane declared. "Look—she knows us already!"

Certainly the mare seemed at ease now. She blew gently into Jeremy's ear as he patted her neck.

"We'll have to think of a name for her," said Jeremy. "We hadn't thought of having a mare really, had we? We'd got names like Tim, and Joker . . ."

"I think her name ought to be Fallada," said Jane

decidedly. "That's an Arab name for a horse in a fairy story I read." She caught sight of Jeremy's expression and added hastily, "Not exactly a fairy story, it was a sort of Arab legend really—and she's beautiful enough to be an Arab anyway."

If Jeremy had had any ideas for a name he might have argued with Jane, but he had to admit that the name suited the pony.

"It's a little bit of a mouthful," he said consideringly. "Let's make it just 'Falla', shall we? I think you're right about Arabs," he added hastily. "I think she's got Arab blood in her, definitely, but where it came from I can't think!"

"Falla . . . Falla," said Jane thoughtfully. "Yes, that's all right."

"Okay, that's settled," said Jeremy. "We'd better find Mr. Hutchinson and see when he'll be ready to take her back."

Jane gave Falla a last pat and turned with Jeremy.

"He was over near the entrance," she began. "Let's tell Uncle Leslie. Oh, he's talking to someone."

Their uncle was talking to a small, very dark man. Jeremy recognised him as one of the men whom he had seen over the other side of the ring during the bidding. The man seemed to be trying to persuade Uncle Leslie to do something. He was talking in a foreign language and gesticulating animatedly. The two children came up and waited until he had finished speaking. It was a language that vaguely reminded Jeremy of French and Latin, yet it wasn't either. The word "*caballo*" seemed to occur quite often, but they spoke too fast for Jeremy to be able to pick out any other words.

Uncle Leslie was shaking his head. "No," he kept on saying. It was almost like the English "No", and its meaning was obvious, but the small dark man continued to plead. Then Uncle Leslie held up his hand with an air of finality.

"No!" he said firmly once more, and added a long sentence that finished with the words: "*los niños*", and he smiled at Jeremy and Jane.

"Ready?" he said to them, and then turned back to the dark man. He made a longish speech in the foreign language, gesturing towards Jeremy and Jane at intervals and speaking in firm tones. At last the dark man raised his shoulders in a gesture of hopelessness, stepped back and bowed.

"What did he want?" asked Jane as they moved off towards the entrance.

Uncle Leslie scratched his head.

"He wanted your pony!" he said bluntly. "Offered me the promise of double what I had paid if I would meet his—well, Principal was the word he used. When I said the mare wasn't for sale he nearly turned himself inside out trying to persuade me. But you came along and then he stopped."

"We wouldn't sell her for hundreds and hundreds of pounds—not ever!" declared Jane.

"I rather gathered that!" Uncle Leslie grinned.

Jeremy glanced back as they turned the corner towards the entrance. The dark man hadn't moved. He was staring after them as if he wanted to make sure he would know them again. Just for a moment Jeremy felt cold . . . but then he brushed the feeling aside. There was nothing anyone could do now—Falla was theirs!

CHAPTER FOUR

TWO REMARKABLE DISCOVERIES

MR. AND Mrs. Fortune were not altogether pleased that Jeremy and Jane had bought a completely unbroken pony. At first they were worried in case the children had taken on too much, especially as Leslie had received a telegram and had had to go off on one of his Interpol jobs, so was not available to help with the breaking in. Also a neighbour of theirs had been at the auction and had brought back the story of Falla's rearing.

Mrs. Fortune tried to persuade the children to get some professional help in the breaking in, but she was met with an indignant refusal.

"We want to have her all to ourselves from the very start," Jeremy explained patiently.

"And she *never* rears now anyway," said Jane. "It was only that she didn't like being chivvied around. Now she knows she belongs to us she's as quiet and gentle as anything. Aren't you, Falla?"

They were all standing in the water meadow watching the grey as she cropped the grass. At the sound of her name she raised her head and trotted over. She nudged Jane gently and blew into the palm of her hand.

"You see?" said Jane, stroking the velvet nose.

"I put a halter on her this morning and she let me lead her all round the field as good as gold," Jeremy added.

Mr. Fortune sighed resignedly.

"All right, then," he said. "But I want you both to promise that you won't ride her out on the roads until your uncle, or Miss Long or someone responsible has watched you and said it's safe."

The children readily agreed to this. In any case Miss Long had offered them the use of the riding school paddock for training Falla.

For the first week or so the children took turns in lungeing Falla round the exercise ring, first to the right and then to the left, with the long lungeing rein buckled to a ring of the snaffle bridle. Falla had given no trouble when the bit was introduced into her mouth. She played about with it at first, but she was soon used to it.

They started her off at a walk round the ring, then, with the voice and a light touch of the whip on her quarters, they urged her to trot. But even the whip wasn't needed more than once, for she quickly learned to respond to the children's voices—"Trot!" spoken in a sharpish tone, and "Whoa!" spoken gently on a falling note.

Then, while Jane gentled her head, Jeremy placed a blanket gently over her withers to accustom her to something on her back. He placed a long girth over the blanket, pulled it under her and passed the end through the buckle, gradually tightening it. Falla twisted her head round and nuzzled his shoulder, then turned back to Jane again and heaved a sigh, as if to say "I don't know what he's playing at, but let him get on with it!"

The next thing was to get her accustomed to the saddle. She did start a little when it was first lowered on to her back, probably because it felt cold, but she quietened at Jane's voice.

"It's a perfect fit," Jeremy said with satisfaction.

"She didn't mind one little bit," said Jane. "J., can't I sit on her back just once?"

"I don't see why not," said Jeremy. "Get up gently, though."

"'Course I will!" said Jane indignantly. She caught the reins, put one foot in the stirrup iron, and was in the saddle like a feather blown there.

"Let go her head. I'll be O.K." she said.

With some misgivings Jeremy let go, remembering that only a few short weeks ago Falla had never even been near a human being. But Jane seemed quietly confident.

"Come on, Falla," she said, squeezing her legs in to the horse's side.

Falla took a hesitant step forward, then another, and the next moment was striding round the ring with her lovely free action. Jane sat very still, her hands just in contact with Falla's mouth. Then she shortened the reins and said clearly: "Trot!"

Falla's head went up at the understood command, but Jane kept her hands low and the reins shortened as Falla trotted round the ring, going just a little unevenly and inclined to shake her head. But on the second circuit she moved more collectedly and did not attempt to snatch at the bit. She stopped at once on the word "Whoa!" and the faintest touch on her mouth.

"See?" said Jane when they stopped. "She comes to hand perfectly—she really *wants* to do the things we tell her!"

By the time another month had passed Falla was walking, trotting and cantering collectedly round the ring. She changed leading leg neatly on a figure-of-eight course too, and seemed to have—as Jane had said—a real desire to please her young owners. When she was asked to do something new she first of all pricked her ears, and if she got it right and was rewarded with a pat on her neck she gave a sort of gay little dance—the smallest of bucks that no more than jogged the rider in the saddle.

By the time the Christmas holidays came the children

had been given permission to take Falla out as much as they liked.

It was early spring before they heard again from their Uncle Leslie. There had been a spell of sunshine with a good drying wind, and the ground in the paddock had improved so much that Miss Long had put up some jumps. The children spent quite a bit of time at week-ends schooling Falla in the ring and putting her over the small jumps.

Uncle Leslie turned up one day towards the end of a session. Jeremy was riding, and when he saw his uncle he proceeded to put Falla through all her paces, finishing up with an immaculate figure of eight with correct leg changes.

"Isn't she gorgeous?" said Jane proudly as she stood watching beside her uncle. "We've been grooming and grooming her. At least," she added honestly, "Jeremy did most of it, because it's awful hard work grooming properly."

"Jane's lazy about that!" Jeremy grinned as he came up to them and slid off Falla's back. "You going to show Uncle Leslie too?"

Jane nodded. "Only to prove she goes just as well for either of us," she said.

Jeremy watched her as she trotted off. She checked Falla at the end of the field, turned her, and put her into a collected trot back. Then they saw her settle down a little in the saddle and across the field heard her make her own special chirrupping noise. Falla's ears twitched backwards to catch the sound, and . . .

"Good lord!" cried Uncle Leslie, watching Falla coming towards them. "How did you teach her to do that?"

Falla was still trotting, but had changed her action to the most peculiar dancing gait. Her foreleg was extended nearly straight forward from the shoulder for every step, and her rear hooves too were lifted high like a show hackney's. With her arched neck and flaring nostrils she looked like one of the horses in a statue group which Jeremy had seen in London.

Falla only did this for a few steps, and then Jane spoke to her again. At once Falla resumed the normal trotting action, and as they pulled up Jane leant forward and patted her neck, while Falla responded with her little gentle dance of joy.

"How did you teach her that?" Uncle Leslie asked again as Jane dismounted.

"I didn't have to," said Jane. "She just naturally does it when I chirrup. I don't know why. I think she likes it."

"Why—is it such a strange thing?" asked Jeremy.

Uncle Leslie's face was solemn.

"That, my children, is called the Spanish trot. It's one of the first *haute école* movements taught—first the walk, then the trot. I've never in all my life known a horse do it naturally without being taught."

"But Falla's a very special horse," said Jane. "She *likes* dancing!"

"But she's always gone awfully collected," Jeremy put in. "She never gets out of hand. Even when she plays up she still stays with us, if you understand what I mean, Uncle Leslie."

His uncle nodded.

"Yes, I do understand. And I agree with Jane—she's exceptional! Mind if I try her?"

"Of course. She'll love having a really super rider like you," said Jeremy.

Falla did seem to appreciate it, too. She arched her neck and danced a little—not playing up, but rather as if she were proud of herself. She went through all the collected paces for him, but he was not able to make her perform her Spanish trot.

"You have to make a special noise," explained Jane. She chirruped to Falla, who pricked up her ears and came towards her. She did take one of the peculiarly high steps, but then stopped dead, snatching at her bit and shaking her head.

"O.K., leave it," called their uncle. "Good girl, Falla, then." He dismounted and gentled her neck. "You see, she hasn't really been taught to do it—it seems a sort of instinct, and she's worried if Jane isn't on her back when she does it."

"That's right. I can't make her do it either," said Jeremy.

"She shows off with me," said Jane. "It's nothing I do specially. How long are you staying this time, Uncle Leslie?"

"Only a few days," said their uncle ruefully. "But I shan't be away long this time, before I'm back again—if you follow me!"

Their uncle worked with them on Falla's training for the time he was there, and they were quick to profit from his advice and experience. By the time the Easter holidays came they were realising that it was true, as Jane said, that they had a really exceptional animal. Miss Long often asked Jeremy or Jane to demonstrate points of dressage to other children learning to ride, and sometimes quite a crowd collected as Falla proudly went through her paces, always finishing with her happy little bucking movement.

The children often went out for the day, taking sandwiches for their lunch. They would arrange to meet somewhere, and one would ride Falla across country while the other cycled to the spot by road, then they would change for the journey back.

It was towards the end of the holidays, during a spell of fine warm weather, that they decided to go to their favourite spot for one of these picnics. It was a clearing near the top of a wooded slope and the beauty of it was that the approach was through a long, straight ride through the trees with soft pine needles underfoot.

"She's been doing a lot of collected work in the ring lately," said Jeremy. "It'll do her good to have a real pipe-opening gallop through the wood. Shall we toss for who rides there and who back?"

"You can have first ride," said Jane magnanimously. "Because of you-know-what."

Jeremy nodded gratefully. They didn't refer very much to the fact that he had to go back to school to-morrow while Jane had one extra day for her school holiday, but he appreciated the kind thought.

The next day Jeremy arrived first at the clearing on the hill-top, after a wonderful gallop through the woods. Jane had started before he had, and in fact he had passed her on the way, so he knew it would be at least another ten minutes before she came.

He dismounted and loosened Falla's girth. She was warm from the brisk gallop, so he led her round the clearing at a walk while she cooled off.

They were just by their usual picnic spot when Falla suddenly snorted and shied.

"What's up, Falla?" Jeremy turned to her in surprise. She was pulling away from him, her ears pricked, staring at something on the ground. He followed the direction of her gaze.

"Don't be silly. It's only a handkerchief that someone's left behind. No, it isn't, it's a sort of scarf. Keep still while I pick it up!"

But Falla backed away, snorting, and wouldn't let him get near the end of white cloth he could see in the bushes. Luckily Jane turned up at that moment, and Jeremy called out to her.

"Come and hold Falla—she doesn't like the look of this scarf thing here."

Jane took hold of Falla's bridle and led her a little way off, looping the reins over a low branch, while Jeremy crawled into the bushes to retrieve the scarf. She had just finished when his voice came to her, slightly muffled.

"I say—come here will you? This is jolly odd!"

Jane couldn't see Jeremy now, but she followed the sound of his voice through the thick bushes. Then suddenly she was out of them and in a little hollow where the bracken and undergrowth had been trimmed back to make a sort of leafy cabin.

"Gosh, it's like a little cave!" she said. "This is the other side of the hill from our picnic place, isn't it?"

"You're right it is," said Jeremy a little grimly. "Look straight ahead—down there."

Jane did so—then gasped. For the bushes had been cut back and arranged to provide a sort of frame for part of the view that lay spread out below them. And the part that was framed was Miss Long's paddock—they could see it quite clearly.

"But," said Jane in a puzzled voice, "I don't understand! Why should anyone want to spy on Miss Long?"

Jeremy scratched his head.

"Beats me," he said. "They've left a scarf behind too." He held up a white scarf, then suddenly sniffed. "D'you smell something—cigarette smoke?" He bent down and pounced on something. "Look, this is it! A cigarette end—and it's only just been put out—see that little speck still glowing? Whoever it was left only a few minutes ago!"

CHAPTER FIVE

JANE GETS A FRIGHT

BY COMMON consent both the children held their breaths and listened. But there were only the little sounds of the wood—the hum of insects and the comfortable tearing sound as Falla cropped the grass in the clearing behind them.

"Well, whoever it was has gone now," said Jeremy at last.

"What'll we do with the scarf?" said Jane.

"Better leave it here," said Jeremy. "They'll probably come back for it, and it wouldn't get taken by anyone else, because no one could find that hidey-hole unless they were looking for it."

"But why should anyone watch the riding school?" said Jane for the second time as they crawled back to their own picnic place again.

"P'raps they were watching us training Falla. Now that would really give them something to look at!" she finished proudly.

Jeremy grunted, but a disquieting thought had struck him. He was remembering back to the day of the Sale—and the little dark man who had tried to buy back Falla. He remembered that the man had been wearing a white silk scarf—it had made his skin look even darker. Jeremy opened his mouth to mention this, then stopped. He didn't want to alarm Jane.

"Shall we go somewhere else for our picnic?" he said instead. "I mean—in case the person comes back for his scarf?"

"Oh, no!" said Jane. "I like it here—and Falla's just found a beautiful patch of clover to eat.

Jeremy put the whole thing out of his mind and stretched himself out on his stomach in the warm grass. From this vantage point he studied Falla's hooves and announced:

"That near fore wants seeing to—there's a nail working loose. Can you take her down to the blacksmith to-morrow?"

Jane nodded.

"All right. I'll go straight after breakfast," she promised. "Then you'll be able to have a ride after your paper round."

After their lunch they spent a happy couple of hours stalking squirrels. To their great joy one of them took a piece of crust off the end of a long stick before dashing away up a tree.

Jeremy was just packing the things into the saddle-bag on the bicycle when he remembered the scarf and the camp in the bushes. On an impulse he dived back into the thicket and came out into the small space again.

It was still empty; in fact it was emptier than before—for the scarf had gone!

"So what?" said Jane when he told her. "They could have come up the other side of the hill, the steep way, couldn't they?"

Jeremy admitted that that was possible, and tried to shake off the uneasy feeling that he had whenever he thought about that silk scarf. It was Jane who usually had odd feelings about things, and she was quite unbothered this time.

The next morning, with all the familiar bustle of getting ready for school, other thoughts were put out of his head; but he did remember to remind Jane about the blacksmith.

She was a little later than she had expected to be, because Falla had had a good roll in some mud during the night and Jane found it was hard work getting it off. It was nearly ten o'clock before she slipped the saddle on Falla and clopped down the lane to Joe Marlow, the blacksmith.

She heard the hissing of hot metal in water and the clang of hammer on anvil as she went in the yard. Joe Marlow was just shoeing a huge cart horse, and he flourished the enormous shoe he held in his tongs at Jane as she came in.

"Bring 'er in, Miss Jane," he said. He looked with approval at Falla's muscles as Jane slipped the halter over her bridle. "She'm a fair treat now—how do she go?"

"Like a bird," Jane told him. "I do think we're lucky. And I think you're a dear to give us her shoes like you did, too."

"She don't need shoeing to-day, though, do she? Just that near fore tidying up, I reckon."

He ran a hand down Falla's leg and lifted her foot. Quickly he clipped off the offending nail and put in another.

"Funny thing 'appened just afore you come," he went on, putting Falla's foot down gently. "Some queer chap, couldn't 'ardly talk the Queen's English 'e couldn't, come in 'ere and says 'Is this the blacksmith?'—leastways, I think that's what 'e meant. Then 'e asks if there's any more round 'ere and I says no, I reckon I'm the only one 'ereabouts. 'E was dressed in some sort of fancy riding togs, so I asks 'im if 'e wants a 'orse shod. 'E didn't seem to know what that meant, so I showed 'im my boot, see, and that seemed to scare 'im proper, some'ow." Joe scratched his head with a horny finger in a puzzled way. "'E shot orf down the road like as if 'e'd fleas in 'is fancy pants, and got into a car—so I reckon the only 'orses 'e knows are under the bonnet. Haw! Haw! Haw!"

Jane giggled delightedly too—she could just imagine how the sight of Joe's number twelve boot waved in anyone's face could be alarming.

"I'd better be going—it's getting on for dinner-time,"

she said, undoing Falla's headstall and leading her round. "Thank you, Joe, and tell little Peggy I've got a surprise for her birthday next week. I can tell *you* what it is, though —I've dressed a doll for her."

Joe's face split in a large grin. Peggy was the youngest of his children, and anything done for her was a sure way to his heart.

"I won't tell her, Miss—not what it is, only that it's a surprise," he promised.

Jane mounted Falla and trotted back up the lane, turning to wave at Joe.

Suddenly Falla shied violently. She couldn't blame the pony because a small, dark man had suddenly appeared from the entrance to a side lane and stepped out into the road right in her path.

"You frightened my horse, coming out suddenly like that," began Jane, then checked.

For another small man had materialised from the side of the road, and they were standing one on each side of her.

Jane looked from one to the other—then spoke to the first one.

"I know you—you spoke to my uncle at the sale last year," she said. "What're you doing here?"

It was the man on the other side who answered her. He spoke English, though with a very strong foreign accent.

"I come to ask you to sell this mare," he said quietly. "You would be wise to do so, since you are not her right owner."

"That's silly!" said Jane spiritedly. She didn't feel frightened—yet. Being on Falla's back above their level gave her confidence. "My Uncle Leslie bought her for us, and we paid him back. It was quite fair!"

"There is one who has a greater claim to her," said the

small man. "And a greater need, too, than any . . . *children.*"

There was a kind of cold dislike in the way he spoke the last word, and Jane felt a little shiver run down her back. He went on:

"But he is a wise and generous man, this person. He will not take without paying, even though it is rightfully his. He will give a fair price."

And he reached inside his jacket and pulled out a wallet full of notes.

Jane looked from the rustling paper to his dark, crafty face, and then at the other small man. Suddenly she felt really frightened. She could feel danger all around her—danger for Falla.

She reacted like lightning to the feeling by giving Falla a sharp tap with her heels behind the girth. The little mare, unused to more than a gentle pressure, bounded forward, and the two men, taken by surprise, stumbled back.

But before Falla could take a second bound Jane heard a strange noise. It was almost the same noise that she herself made to horses—the soft chirruping—but with a different inflection—more urgent, somehow. Falla heard it too, for she checked almost in mid-air and spun round with a movement so rapid that Jane was almost unseated.

Then Falla stood stock still with her ears pricked forward and her gentle, intelligent eyes fixed on the second dark little man—the one who had not spoken so far.

He was still making that strange little noise, and Falla suddenly blew out through her nostrils and took a hesitant step towards him, then another as if she were hypnotised.

Jane, frantic now, laid the reins against Falla's neck and urged her to turn with her leg, but Falla, usually so obedient to the aids, took no notice. She went on advancing towards the little dark man. Another few steps and he would be able to grasp her bridle.

Jane gave a little sob.

"Falla!" she gasped. "Oh, Falla!"

But then there was a sudden flurry of noise behind them—a jingling of many bicycle bells and the sound of shouting and laughter. And round the corner of the lane behind them swung a bunch of cyclists—obviously a cycling club out on a run.

And it broke the spell. Falla's head at last came round in obedience to Jane's hands and heel, and before the last cyclist was out of sight Jane had clapped her heels to Falla's sides and was streaking down the lane for the safety of the riding school.

Falla too seemed to understand that they were escaping from something, for she went like lightning, and turned into the cart track leading to the riding school of her own accord.

When the stables were in sight Jane pulled up from her headlong gallop. A glance behind her showed that the two men had made no attempt to follow, and she gentled Falla down to a walk while she tried to think things out.

Why, she thought, why should they want Falla so badly? She was only a New Forest pony after all, even though she was so good-looking. True, she was a grey, which was unusual—but that wouldn't make her anything particularly wonderful.

In the yard of the riding school there was a crowd of youngsters on ponies just starting off for a ride with Miss Long in charge. She waved to Jane as she came through the gateway.

"Coming with us?" she called.

Jane nodded.

"Yes, please," she said, turning Falla round. She felt the need for company, and with her friends round her she could put off her puzzling thoughts for the moment. All the same, during the ride she kept a sharp lookout, but there was no sign of the two men—they seemed to have vanished completely.

But when they returned she buttonholed Miss Long.

"Please, may I ask you a favour?" she said.

Miss Long smiled at her serious face.

"I should think you might!" she said cheerfully. "What is it?"

"May I leave Falla here in one of your empty stalls—just till Jeremy comes back from school—instead of taking her home?" Jane begged.

Miss Long shot her a sharp glance.

"Of course you can, dear," she said. "But why? Is there something wrong?"

"I—I'm not sure," said Jane. "But d'you mind if I don't tell you until I've talked to Jeremy about it?"

Miss Long lifted one eyebrow, but she didn't say any more except: "All right. Put her in the end stall. That's not being used for the time being."

Jane tied up Falla, rubbed her down and borrowed someone's bicycle to fetch some of Falla's hay from the shed in the water meadow.

Jeremy always did his paper round straight after school, and then came home. Jane was waiting by the gate for him as he arrived.

"J., have you got any homework? I want you to come up to Miss Long's after tea—it's rather important."

"No," Jeremy answered her first question. "Why, what's up?"

"I'll tell you as we go," said Jane. "I don't think Mummy and Daddy ought to know about it."

Jeremy, curious and a little apprehensive, finished his tea in record time and changed into his jodhpurs.

"Come on, out with it!" he said as they went out of the gate. He started off towards the water meadow. "We'll get Falla first and take her up there."

"She's there already," Jane told him. "Because of what happened, you see." And she told Jeremy the whole story.

Jeremy listened silently, his face solemn.

"It all fits in," he said at last. "Don't you see, that place on top of the hill is where they've been watching us training Falla at the riding school—without our knowing, too. And that scarf that vanished! When they came to fetch it they must have heard us arranging for you to go to the blacksmith in the morning."

"What are we going to do?" wailed Jane.

Jeremy considered.

"They seem to want Falla—but for some reason they want to buy her properly," he said. "But for the moment I think it'd be best if you didn't go out alone with her—go with the school for a while."

Jane nodded.

"I'll do that," she said. "And let's tell Miss Long about it, too. Perhaps—perhaps we ought to tell the police, too?"

"Tell them what?" said Jeremy. "That a man offered to buy Falla and then hypnotised her? They just wouldn't believe you. I do, of course!" he added hastily as Jane's lower lip trembled.

"W-what about you?" she asked.

"Oh, I'll be all right—I'm pretty well as big as they are anyway! Buck up, Janey, we'll tell Miss Long, at any rate."

But when they arrived at the riding school they were greeted by Mary, the girl who was employed there.

"Miss Long's only just gone," she said. "She had a phone call—got to go up north for a week or two," she said.

"But she left a message for you two. You can leave Falla here for a couple of nights if you want to, but there are two new liveries coming in on Friday, so she can't stay after that."

Jeremy looked at Jane, who caught at his arm.

"Let's do that," she whispered. "We needn't say why."

Jeremy turned back to Mary.

"Thanks—thanks awfully," he said. "We would like to leave her here till Friday if we can. Her meadow could do with a rest from being grazed, and I want to do some work on the shed too."

That evening when Jeremy had returned from his ride they talked things over again.

"I didn't see anyone suspicious," he reported. "In fact I had the country to myself. And I did a bit of thinking—and what I thought was this. It's quite true that the water meadow needs a rest. It won't hurt Falla to keep her up for a while, but we can't keep her at Miss Long's after Friday, even if we could afford it. Now it's quite possible that those two men don't know that we keep Falla in the water meadow—they may only have been watching the riding school and seen us in and out of there. But just for safety I'm going to put a good padlock on the shed door, and we'll keep Falla in except when we're there to watch her."

"We could give her an hour's grazing night and morning—there's plenty of roadside grass," Jane said. "And you need only padlock the bottom half of the door, then she'll be able to look out. But—how long d'you think it'll go on?"

"Well, d'you know I think it's jolly likely they've given up already," said Jeremy. "But let's keep her in till Uncle Leslie comes down next week. He'll know what to do!"

"Yes, so he will!" Jane spoke with relief. "But if those

horrid men have got any sense they must know that there's no chance of our selling Falla. It's just that we must take all reasonable pro-pro-cautions."

"It's *pre*-cautions," Jeremy couldn't resist telling her.

In spite of their brave words, however, both Jeremy and Jane were uneasy. Jeremy worked on the shed one evening and strengthened the door, fixing a strong padlock on to the lower half. Jane got up early and gave Falla her feed and some grazing before breakfast. When she exercised Falla she kept to the school paddock and did not go out on the roads.

But on Friday afternoon, when Jeremy came home he found Jane waiting for him, beaming all over her face.

"They've gone! They've gone right away!" she said, giving a little skip.

Jeremy didn't need to ask whom she meant. The two sinister little dark men were never far from his thoughts.

"How do you know? Are you sure?"

"Quite sure! You see, it was because of this doll I've been dressing for Peggy Marlow's birthday. I finished it yesterday evening and took it down at lunch-time to-day. Joe was there, and we got talking, and he said to me: 'D'you remember that furrin bloke wot asked me if I was the only blacksmith 'ereabouts?' and I said 'Yes, I did'."

"Get on with it!" said Jeremy, trying not to grin at Jane's accurate reproduction of Joe Marlow's slow tones.

"Well, Joe said he'd just been 'avin' a pint with Fred Withers up at the Green Man—all right, I am getting on, really Jeremy!—and this foreign chap had been staying there. Two of them, Joe said Fred said . . ." Jane paused for breath, and Jeremy, realising he would have to let her tell it at her own pace, said, "Go on!" resignedly.

"Then Joe said Fred said they'd left that very morning—to-day that'd be, you see—and it was all an awful fuss and bother because they hadn't enough money to meet their bill! At least they said they hadn't—but one of the maids piped up and said she'd seen them take out a wallet bulging with notes, and Fred noticed one of the little men's pockets looked rather fat and taxed him with it. And in the end he pulled out this wallet and paid up, but jolly crossly, Joe said Fred said!"

"You're getting me muddled with all these 'saids'," complained Jeremy.

"And this is the important part," said Jane. "Joe said Fred said—if you make a face like that, J., I won't tell you!" She took a deep breath. " '*If those two jokers ever show their ugly mugs in this part of the world again I'll 'ave 'em run right out so their feet don't touch the ground!*' "

Jeremy did a sort of war-dance right there in the lane. "Gosh, that's wonderful!" he said. "We can put Falla back in the water meadow and not worry."

"She's there already," said Jane smugly. "And wolfing back the grass like anything!"

Nothing could damp their spirits after that, even the fact that it started raining that evening and continued without a stop all over the week-end.

But the days went like a flash to the two children, and on Sunday night they both dropped off to sleep as soon as their heads touched the pillow.

It was much later when a sound woke Jeremy. He opened his eyes and blinked. It couldn't be time to get up yet—it was still quite dark, with the window just showing a faint patch of lesser darkness.

Then he heard it again—and in a moment he was wide awake and out of bed.

For the sound that had come to him quite distinctly was Falla whinnying—and she never did that for nothing!

CHAPTER SIX

SUSPICION BECOMES CERTAINTY

JEREMY GLANCED at his luminous alarm clock. The hands said two o'clock. There shouldn't be anyone about at that time to make Falla whinny.

He felt his way over to the window. It was pretty dark, but he knew that his window looked across to the water meadow and the shed. He stood there what seemed like a long time, but there was no further sound.

Then he saw something, just for a second. It was a little pinpoint of light over in the direction of the water meadow. It shone quite distinctly for a moment, and then seemed to disappear.

He hastily slipped on his jeans and a pair of plimsolls—leaving his pyjama top as a shirt. Somehow he knew that speed was important. Then he crept out of his room and paused just to listen at Jane's door. All was quiet—she hadn't heard anything.

He let himself quietly out of the back door and hastily transferred to the grass verge as his foot crunched on the gravel. He was out of the gate and down the lane like a shadow—eyes and ears alert, stifling the cold fear that was trying to grip him.

When he reached the hedge bounding the meadow he went even more carefully, creeping along in the shadow. Everything was quiet.

Then he was at the gate which led into the meadow, and he stopped and peered cautiously through. It was shut, but Jeremy knew that as he went across his moving figure would be visible to anyone looking from the field.

He put his head down and darted across at full speed. The next moment he had cannoned head-on into a man standing at the opposite side of the gateway, silent and invisible. He hit a hard, muscular leg with his lowered head, and collapsed on the ground, counting stars.

"Blow me, what's all this?" said a deep rustic voice above him, and a blinding light was turned on Jeremy, who was sitting on the grass rubbing his head. "Why, if it ain't young Master Fortune! What are you doing outer your bed this time o' night?"

Jeremy blinked at the strong light. He knew the voice well. It was the local constable, Frank Marlow, brother to Joe the blacksmith. Jeremy had never in his whole life been so glad to see Frank's stolid, burly form.

"Gosh, I'm glad it's you!" he said. "Did you see them?"

"See 'oo? There's not been anyone round 'ere to-night."

"Which way did you come, Frank?" Jeremy got up and shook his head to clear it.

"From back there," Frank jerked his head back down the lane. "And not a sight nor sound has there been—barring that horse o' yours that gave a couple of whinnies, like."

"There must have been someone there when she whinnied!" Jeremy gave an impatient hop. "I saw a light flash on too. Really, I did, Frank! From my bedroom window—it'd be the other side of the shed from here."

"Well, we'd best go and look round, seein' as you're agitated, Master Jeremy." Frank slipped the loop off the gate and walked into the field, followed by Jeremy. "Proper wet here, isn't it."

They squelched across the meadow and reached the shed. Falla whinnied as she heard Jeremy's voice, and he called out: "It's all right, Falla—it's only me!"

"Do she understand that?" asked Frank, grinning.

"Of course she do—does!" said Jeremy. "She's a highly intelligent person."

Frank walked all round the shed and tested the padlock.

"Reckon you're mistaken this time, Master Jeremy," he said finally. "Mayhap it was my torch you saw—I had it shining to take a look round, times."

"Perhaps that was it!" Jeremy seized on the explanation with relief. "It was so dark—I might have mistaken the direction quite easily."

At that moment a small figure flung itself into the circle of light from the big bull's-eye torch, and a breathless voice said:

"J., what's up? I heard you step on the path, and I had to follow you. Is—is someone trying to steal Falla?"

"Jane—you shouldn't come out like that with only pyjamas and a dressing gown!" scolded Jeremy. "No, there's nothing wrong. It's only Frank and me. I thought I saw a light, so I came along, but it must have been Frank's torch."

"It's not very likely that anyone would try to steal your horse, Miss Jane," Frank said in his slow voice. "It'd be the fodder and tack more likely they'd want. I should keep it well locked up if I was you."

He tested the padlock once more, then turned away.

"Well, I'd best see you both home—more'n time you was back in bed. And don't you go getting up for no more lights, because it'll likely be the arm of the law on his lawful business!" and he gave a guffaw.

The children joined in, and were glad enough to be escorted back to their home. Frank lighted them up the path to the door with the big beam of his torch, and they crept quietly up to bed.

"I'm glad it was only Frank," Jane whispered, yawning.

Jeremy nodded. He too felt tired now that the tension was over. Everything could be explained. Falla had probably heard Frank's step and whinnied at him—and the light had been his torch.

Uncle Leslie arrived soon after Jeremy got home the next day. The children fell on him with delight.

"Come and see how Falla's looking!"

"Her coat's *beautiful* now!"

"Children! Children! Let the poor man have some tea before you make him tramp round the countryside!" Mrs. Fortune shooed them away. "What about your homework?"

"I've only got some copying."

"And I haven't got any. But I'll read yours out to you so you can copy quicker," offered Jane.

Luckily the finish of Jeremy's homework coincided with their uncle's last cup of tea, so they were able to set off for the water meadow without further delay.

"There's lots of things to tell you," began Jane as they walked down the lane.

Their uncle looked from one serious face to the other.

"Looks as though they aren't very nice things," he said.

"Some of them aren't," admitted Jeremy. "What was the first thing, Jane?"

"That man who talked to Uncle Leslie at the auction," said Jane promptly.

"The Spaniard? But I choked him off. I said the pony definitely wasn't for sale."

"But he wasn't choked off. You see there was the hidey-hole on the hill."

"And the men who stopped me."

"Look here," said Uncle Leslie. "Just start at the beginning. Jeremy, let's hear what you've got to say first."

Jeremy told his uncle about their discovery that someone had been watching the riding school paddock. "If they had field glasses they could see every detail," he said. Then Jane chipped in with her adventure on the way back from the blacksmith's.

"I was scared," she admitted. "You can't imagine how awful it was when Falla just walked towards the man and I couldn't turn her away." She shuddered at the memory.

"It must have been rather frightening," said her uncle. "And one of the men was the man who'd spoken to me at the auction?"

"Yes. He actually didn't talk to me at all, but he was the one who made that funny noise so that Falla went all gooey."

Uncle Leslie looked thoughtful. "What was the noise like?" he asked.

"I can do something like it." Jane gave her chirruping sound. "But it was different—sort of whistly and louder."

Uncle Leslie nodded thoughtfully. "Yes. Well, what happened then?"

"Nothing more, really. The cyclists seemed to break the spell somehow, and I just made for the riding school as fast as I could. I haven't been out on the roads alone since—and Jeremy hasn't met anyone, have you J.?"

"I didn't see anything suspicious at all," said Jeremy. "But we decided to take up Miss Long's offer to keep Falla there until Friday. And then Jane found out that the two men had left."

"Under a cloud!" put in Jane dramatically.

Their uncle laughed at the story of the attempt not to pay the bill at the Green Man.

"You know, it sounds as if that money was what they had to offer you for Falla. They'd spent all the rest they'd got and were supposed to keep it intact," he said.

"They won't dare to come back, anyway—not in the day-time."

"Not in the day-time," echoed Jeremy, then suddenly went a little bit pale.

"Oh, you're thinking about last night," said Jane.

"Last night?" Uncle Leslie pricked up his ears.

"Yes. I heard Falla whinny. It was about two o'clock this morning, actually. And I thought I saw a light in the meadow, so I went out to see."

"And I followed him," added Jane. "But it turned out it was only Frank Marlow—he's the policeman—with his torch doing a night round."

They had reached the gate of the water meadow by now, and Jeremy went on: "I met him about here, and we went in just to have a look round, but everything was quiet. Frank shone his torch . . ."

Jeremy suddenly stopped, and his face went positively green. He sat down abruptly on the ground as what he had been trying to remember came to the top of his mind.

"J., what's the matter? Are you feeling sick?" Jane's worried voice penetrated the mist that he felt round him.

"I've just remembered something," he said in a kind of croak. "The light I saw—it wasn't Frank! It couldn't have been! He had a huge great powerful torch, and this was just a thin little faint beam—like—like a pencil torch with the battery rather worn down!"

Jane fell on to her knees and stared into Jeremy's face in dismay.

"Oh, J., d'you think it was really someone—those two men—trying to steal Falla," she whispered. She turned a white face up to Uncle Leslie. "What shall we do—what *can* we do?"

Uncle Leslie's face was set and stern. The two children had never seen it like that before. He reached down a strong kindly hand and hauled Jeremy to his feet.

"I won't pretend with you two," he said. "There's

something going on—something rather odd that I don't altogether understand myself. But there are a few points that might give me a line to work on—the Spaniard—the Spanish trot—that noise."

"Uncle Leslie, what're you talking about? I can't understand!" cried Jane, shaking his arm. He came out of his abstraction with a start, and gave her a reassuring grin.

"Sorry," he said. "I was thinking aloud. Now, the first thing is to see if we can find any proof that someone *was* here last night. There wasn't anyone when you and the policeman went in, Jeremy?"

Jeremy shook his head. "Frank shone his searchlight all around," he said. "And they couldn't have come out of the gate, either, because we were there."

"Um. Ground's pretty soggy—good for prints," said their uncle, leading the way over to the shed. "Ah—here's Jeremy's print—looks like a rubber sole."

"I'd got plimsolls on," said Jeremy.

"And Jane's—rather indistinct."

"My bedroom slippers," admitted Jane.

"And these must be Frank the policeman's," Uncle Leslie indicated some huge water-filled indentations like small lakes.

"But whose print is this?" Uncle Leslie indicated the mark of sole and heel, separated as though the heel were rather higher than that of an ordinary shoe. "It looks like a riding boot."

"One of the men had breeches and boots!" cried Jane.

"I've found some more!" cried Jeremy, who was walking about with his nose nearly touching the ground. "Just ordinary shoes—small men's, I think. They're leading towards this very boggy patch. Gosh, look!"

He was squatting down, precariously balanced on a tuft of grass, and tugging at something half buried in the mud.

It came up with a loud squelch, and he waved a natty gent's shoe in the air. At least it had been natty—now it was a sorry object festooned with mud and dripping sadly.

"It's a clue—it's a clue!" Jane was dancing up and down excitedly.

"It certainly is! And, if I'm not mistaken, that's the way they went out!" Uncle Leslie pointed over towards the hedge at a line of footprints—a mixture of riding boots, shoes and an odd mark obviously made by a shoeless foot. There were scraps of cloth caught in the prickles too—they hadn't had an easy passage, obviously.

"They must have heard your policeman patrolling and beaten a hasty retreat through here. They'd strike the lane farther along and probably they'd left a car or something back out of earshot," Uncle Leslie went on.

Jeremy suddenly grinned for the first time.

"Gosh, I bet they didn't look as smart when they went as they did when they arrived!"

They all looked at one another and burst out laughing. The picture of the two men limping down the lane, covered in mud and probably scratched from having crawled through the hedge was a bit comic relief in a situation that had threatened to become unpleasant.

"I'm awfully glad you're here, Uncle Leslie," said Jeremy, suddenly sobering. "Because they may come back, mayn't they? Hadn't we better keep guard at night. I mean you and me, not Jane of course."

His uncle nodded.

"I think it'd be a good idea," he said. "But I'll do the guarding if you don't mind." He silenced Jeremy's protest. "Don't be an ass! Your mother would half kill me if I let you stay up all night in school time!"

"But you can't keep awake all night and every night—we don't know how long it'd go on for!"

"If I can follow up a few points—and I think I can—I might be able to get it sorted out fairly soon," said his uncle. "I'm used to night watches, anyway. It's always been part of my job."

"When you've been tracking down criminals?" asked Jane, her eyes round.

"That's right!" He tweaked her snub nose. "But come on—that's enough sleuthing for one evening. Where's this Falla?"

"Oh, my lovely Falla! We'd nearly forgotten about you!" Jane rushed to the shed and unlocked the padlock. "We've kept her in to-day because of all that rain—but the ground's dried out enough for her to be out to-morrow. You don't think they'd come in the day-time, do you, Uncle Leslie?"

"Pretty certain they won't. Everyone knows them now in a small place like this," said her uncle.

They saddled Falla and rode her round to show off her paces. Jane put her into the Spanish trot for a moment, and Jeremy jumped her over a small bush. Then they stood and watched her while she grazed for a while.

"She's pretty handy," observed their uncle. "You two ride her well."

"She's naughty about leading with the off fore sometimes," said Jane. "You have to give her a stronger aid for that side. Perhaps she's left-footed, like people are left-handed sometimes."

"Left-footed!" said Uncle Leslie suddenly. "Yes, that fits too!" He went off into another fit of thinking, watched respectfully by the children.

"Is it a clue?" asked Jane at last in a small voice. Her uncle came back to earth and grinned at her.

"Not exactly," he said. "But it might show that she's got Arab blood—nearly all Arab horses are left-footed. But ome English ones are too," he finished hastily. "So don't nake too much of it!"

"I knew it! I always said she was an Arab!" cried Jane.

"No you didn't. You just said she was beautiful and ıeavenly and all that sort of tripe," put in Jeremy.

"Well, we'd best call it a day," said their uncle pacifically. 'I'm going back to write some letters. You two follow me vhen you've finished." He turned towards the gate. "And leep snug to-night—all night!" he added. "I'll be keeping n eye on things."

The two children did sleep soundly, and were up early he next morning, almost as soon as it was full daylight. They met their uncle just coming into the house.

"Not a sausage!" he reported. "Tell your mother I'll leep till midday, will you? She won't mind—she knows do things at night sometimes."

When the children passed on the message to their mother he smiled reminiscently.

"Leslie's always liked working at night—even when he vas a boy he used to go out fishing and things like that," he said. "He doesn't seem to need as much sleep as most eople. I wonder what he was up to this time?"

Luckily the milk on the stove boiled over, and in the nopping up operations the children were spared the ıecessity of answering.

The week-end passed happily but uneventfully, and also he next three nights. The children were looking forward articularly to the Friday, since they had a day off from chool. The teachers at Jane's school were attending a ecture course held at Jeremy's school, so both children ıad the day free.

On Thursday morning a letter arrived for Uncle Leslie. The children saw it lying on the mat before they went to chool, but their uncle was not up, having just gone to bed.

When they got home that night their mother held out a note.

"Leslie's had to go off somewhere," she told them. "He left this note for you—said it would be too long to leave by word of mouth! What's on? Is it a sort of secret society with you all?"

"Yes, it is, sort of," said Jane. She suddenly threw her arms round her mother. "I expect you and Uncle Leslie had secrets, too, in the olden days," she said seriously.

"You make us sound hundreds of years old!" smiled her mother. "But I know what you mean. Yes, we did!"

The children rushed up to Jeremy's bedroom and sat on the bed to read their uncle's letter.

"Here—you read it to me." Jane thrust it impatiently towards Jeremy. "I can't understand his writing."

"It's quite clear really," said Jeremy loftily. "First of all he says he's got to go to Gloucestershire following up a live . . . something . . . no, it's a line. Following up a line——"

"I thought you said it was easy to read," put in Jane.

"Shut up! A line that might lead to somewhere helpful. Um—doesn't give much away does he! Then he says 'Jeremy, I may not be back to-night. Can you do the watch for me? I wouldn't ask if I thought there was any danger, but even if they do turn up I think the sound or presence of someone would scare them off at once.' "

"Then why can't I do the watching with you?" demanded Jane.

"Listen, he's thought of that. He says: 'Don't let Jane do it. She must promise. If your mother thought I'd let her stay out all night in a field I'd never be allowed to speak to either of you again!' "

Jane subsided. "Oh, dear, yes. Mummy *would* be furious," she said.

"And you don't like the dark when you're alone," Jeremy pointed out. "All right then, that's settled. I'll go to bed and creep out when it's dark. Luckily it gets dark pretty late now, and Mum and Dad go to bed early. Promise you'll stay, Jane."

"I promise," said Jane in a small voice.

"Good!" Jeremy looked at her disappointed face. "Tell you what, though. You set your alarm for very early—about five o'clock. It's light then and you can come out and fetch me. I won't know the time, you see, because I haven't got a watch. Mummy wouldn't mind that, because we've often got up early before."

"All right—I'll do that," said Jane, cheering up.

She didn't mean to drop off to sleep that night. She tried very hard to keep herself awake because she wanted to go over to the window every now and again to see if there was anything doing in the water meadow.

First of all she tried sitting up, but that got rather uncomfortable. Then she lay down, but that was far too sleep-making, so she tried taking away her pillow, and lay there saying through all the poetry she knew and getting up at the end of each poem. But in between the end of one verse and the beginning of the next she blinked, and didn't open her eyes after the blink.

The next thing she knew was the alarm going off. Jane went to dive under the pillow as she usually did in the morning, but there wasn't any pillow and suddenly she remembered. She jumped out of bed, pulled on a jersey and a pair of jeans and picked up her wellingtons to creep downstairs. She put them on in the porch and once out of the gate ran cheerfully down the lane.

But when she came to the gate of the water meadow her heart gave a little thump. For it was open. Perhaps Jeremy had left it open . . . but he never did as a rule.

Then as she went in she saw what she had dreaded to see. Both halves of the shed door were swinging open.

Jane ran towards the shed as fast as her shaking legs would carry her—but there was no escaping the fact—Falla had gone!

Jane glanced panic-stricken round the empty shed. Jeremy! Where was Jeremy was all she could think of for the moment.

"Jeremy!" she called in a frightened squeak. "J., where are you?"

She held her breath and listened but there wasn't a sound.

"Jeremy!" she cried, on a sob now. She ran out of the shed and round the side, calling frantically.

Then she saw him, in the little lean-to at the side of the shed that they used for storing hay. He was stretched out on a pile of hay and looked quite peacefully asleep.

"Oh, poor Jeremy!" thought Jane, gasping with relief. "He must have felt awfully tired and just dropped off like I did."

She knelt down by Jeremy's side and shook him. At that moment she heard hurried footsteps behind her, and her Uncle Leslie's voice.

"Jane! Jeremy!" then a sort of gasp, and something that sounded like "Too late!"

Jane shook Jeremy again, then once more even harder. She turned a white face up to her uncle who stood in the doorway.

"I—I can't wake him up!" she said.

CHAPTER SEVEN

JANE AND JEREMY BEGIN TO UNDERSTAND

UNCLE LESLIE knelt down beside Jeremy and picked up his wrist. After a moment he laid a hand on Jeremy's orehead, then he looked over to Jane with a sigh of relief.

"He'll be all right," he said. "I think he's been drugged —but he'll come round before long." He turned up the leeve of Jeremy's blue jersey and pointed to a pin-prick ark on his upper arm.

"That's it—they gave him a shot to keep him quiet," he old her. His face was grim now—grim and unrelenting. They'll pay for this," he said quietly.

But Jane wasn't listening. Now that she knew Jeremy as not seriously hurt the full realisation of what had appened came over her.

"They've taken Falla!" she cried. "Uncle Leslie, she's one! The door was open when I got here——"

She scrambled to her feet, and after a glance at Jeremy, Jncle Leslie followed her. He examined the idly-swinging oor.

"They unscrewed the padlock," he said. "That'd be the uietest way of course." He walked into the shed and lanced round. "Hallo—what's this?" he called suddenly.

Jane followed him in and looked where he indicated. here, lying in the rough wooden trough which they used s a manger, was a bundle of treasury notes, anchored by a arge stone.

Uncle Leslie picked them out. "There must be about eventy pounds here," he said.

Tears were streaming down Jane's face.

"They wanted to pay me before!" she sobbed. "The th-think it's all right to take her if they pay me for her— but it isn't! I wouldn't sell Falla for any money in th world."

Uncle Leslie put his arm round her shoulders.

"Don't cry, Janey," he said. "We'll get Falla back fo you—I promise!"

Jane looked up at him, her tears checked for the momen

"Why? D'you know where she is?" she asked with gulp.

"N-no, not exactly," he admitted. "But I think I ca probably find out and I'm pretty sure she's safe and wel cared for. But right now the important thing is to ge Jeremy back home and into bed. Come along!"

Jeremy hadn't moved, but as his uncle bent over to lif him up his eyes opened. He blinked rapidly several times then struggled into a sitting position.

"Uncle Leslie! How did you get here? Gosh! Have been asleep?" he stopped abruptly, and Jane could see tha his memory was returning.

"Where are they?" he half shouted, trying to get up "Falla—is she all right?"

His uncle pressed him firmly down again.

"Don't worry, old man. I'm afraid they took Falla. Bu they had to put you out of the way first. Now I'm going t carry you back home."

"I can walk all right," said Jeremy, pushing aside hi uncle's arm and staggering to his feet. He collapse suddenly into the hay. "Oh, bother! My legs have gone a rubbery!"

"Then you'll have to put up with my giving you a lift, said his uncle. "Now"—as Jeremy began to speak again— "don't talk for the moment. Later I want to hear wha happened—every little detail that you can remember—so start thinking now, will you?"

Mrs. Fortune was up and had just put on the kettle when they got in. Her face went white when she saw them—Jeremy in his uncle's arms and Jane with her face streaked with tears and dirt where she had rubbed her eyes.

"What's happened? Leslie, is he hurt?"

"It's all right, Meg—honestly it is." Leslie put Jeremy down gently on the old sofa in the corner, where he promptly sat up and reassured his mother who was hovering over him anxiously.

"Really, I'm all right, Mummy. I'm just feeling a bit dopey."

Mrs. Fortune felt Jeremy's forehead and gave a quick glance at his eyes, which were bright and alert now, and his colour which had returned to normal. Then her lips tightened and she turned back to her brother.

"I think you'd better do some explaining," she said in a cold voice. "And it had better be . . ."

At that moment the kettle boiled over and put out the gas, and somehow this relieved the tension, for she let out her breath in a sigh.

"I'll make tea for all of us," she said. "Janey, go and tell your father to come down. He ought to hear about this too."

She made the tea. The others watched her, and nobody spoke a word until Jane appeared with her father in tow, still wiping the shaving soap from his face.

"I don't know what all this is about," he said irritably. "Jane drags me out of the bathroom saying that their horse has been stolen. Will someone explain, please?"

Mrs. Fortune set another cup of tea on the table.

"Sit down, John—and we'll all listen to the explanation," she said quietly. "Now, Leslie——"

"I'd better start at the beginning, Meg—even thougl Jeremy and Jane know the first part of it," he said. "I suppose it started at the Sale . . ."

He told about the Spaniard approaching him and tryin to buy Falla; then he went on to relate all the incident that had happened up to date. His police training enable him to put the whole story in a clear, logical fashion, an the children listened in silence too. But when he mentione his note for Jeremy, Mrs. Fortune interrupted for the firs time.

"Leslie, you shouldn't have let that child stay up al night with dangerous criminals about! It was wicked o you!" she cried.

"Meg, I'm truly sorry about that," he answered humbly "I misjudged things badly. First of all I didn't think they'c go even that far . . . and also I thought I'd be in time t stop anything happening at all."

"And they weren't really dangerous!" Jeremy's voic came strongly now. "They had to stop me making a nois or raising an alarm—but they never tried to hurt me! The could have hit me over the head instead of injectin something——"

"Let's hear exactly what happened to you," his fathe interrupted.

Jeremy swung his feet to the ground and stood up experimentally. "My legs are as good as ever now," he announced. "All right, Mum, I'll sit down again, don't fuss! Now, let me think. Oh, yes. It was all quiet for ages at first, and I got rather bored. I could hear Falla guzzling hay, but I didn't talk to her because of not making a noise. After a bit it got colder, so I went into the little place at the side of the shed where we keep the hay, and I sat on a bale and looked out from there."

"Did you go to sleep?" asked Jane.

"No jolly fear! I was on guard," said Jeremy indignantly. 'But I never heard them come. I think they must have valked round the edge of the field where it's dry. All I saw vas the doorway suddenly grow dark, and then they were n each side of me, and one had a hand clapped over my nouth. I tried to bite him, and I think I caught him a bit, ecause he gave a sort of grunt and muttered something I ouldn't understand—it might have been Spanish again, nightn't it, Uncle Leslie?"

His uncle nodded. "Go on," he said.

"I was kicking and struggling of course, but they were wfully strong. Then I suppose they realised that they vouldn't be able to keep me quiet, because one of them aid something else in Spanish, and pulled up the sleeve of my jersey, while the other shone a little pencil torch on ny arm. Then something pricked me and—and—that's all emember, until I saw Uncle Leslie this morning," Jeremy inished rather shame-facedly.

"I don't understand why the horse didn't make a noise," aid his father.

"It's those men—they can sort of hypnotise her," said ane decidedly. "That proves it!" She turned to her uncle. 'Uncle Leslie! You said you thought you knew where 'alla was and you said you didn't think they'd go that far."

"Yes, Leslie," said her father. "I've got the feeling that ou know more about this affair than you've let out so far."

"I do know more—now," he said. "Until yesterday it was ll guesswork. That's why I went away yesterday—up to Gloucestershire." He paused for a moment. "It's a pretty ong story—and it goes back about seven years. Jane, you tarted me off on the trail. You remember you mentioned hat circus where the grey Arab horse 'danced' as you put t?" Jane nodded. "Now, ever since you've had Falla, hings have reminded me of him. Her appearance, the way she performed the Spanish trot—a movement that she could never have been taught—then those two Spaniards and the way they could almost hypnotise her with that sound they made. And I remembered all I knew about Ramiro Toral and his Arab stallion, Brioso, that must be getting on in years now.

"So I wrote to the head of the chain of circuses where I had last heard of Ramiro performing, and I got a reply yesterday morning, from Landers, the owner. It said he was glad to hear from a friend of Ramiro. Apparently he was anxious to re-engage him for the summer circus season but had received nothing but evasive replies to his letters. And he asked if I would go and see Ramiro and find out if I could what the position was, and let him know.

"I had the feeling that in Gloucestershire I would find the answer to the puzzling things that had been happening here. So I wasted no time in getting there, and I found the farm where Ramiro was staying." Leslie's voice stopped and they could all see that he was troubled.

"Please go on, Uncle Leslie," said Jane in a small voice. "Was he ill?"

"No—no, he wasn't physically ill," said her uncle slowly. "He just seemed to have changed—grown harder. He was a very charming person always, but there was uneasiness in his glance somehow. He wouldn't meet my eyes.

"I asked after his horse, the great Brioso, which at one time was famous all over the world. 'He grows old and has a lameness in his shoulder,' he told me. 'But his spirit is as great as ever.' He took me out to see the old chap. He's a beauty all right, pure white now, but lovely conformation and carriage.

" 'He is not really fit to work more,' Ramiro told me. 'But I shall have another very soon now. Even though she is a mare I shall take her to train. It is reported to me that she shows exceptional talent already, and under my tuition she will worthily follow her great sire, my old friend Brioso here.' "

"Did he—did he mean Falla?" said Jeremy in an awed whisper.

Uncle Leslie nodded.

"Yes—Falla," he said.

"But, how could Brioso be her sire?" asked Jeremy. "She was born in the New Forest—I thought her parents were both New Forest ponies."

"Go on, Uncle Leslie, did Mr. Ramiro tell you what had happened?" said Jane.

Uncle Leslie nodded again.

"It was about four years ago," he said. "Ramiro and Brioso had given a guest performance at a circus in Southampton and they were travelling overnight to Birmingham. The driver of the horse-box had taken one drink too many, and he had a glancing collision with a car while they were travelling through the New Forest. The horse-box careered off the road, crashed into the ditch and was completely wrecked. The driver was killed, and Ramiro was flung out and badly concussed. Brioso must have scrambled out somehow from the wreckage and galloped off into the Forest, pretty well crazy with fear.

"Ramiro woke up the next day in hospital. Of course, the first question he asked was about Brioso, and he learnt to his horror that they had found no trace of him in the wreckage. You can imagine that Ramiro wasn't the best of patients after that. Long before he was officially allowed out of bed he was off, searching the New Forest, calling for his horse."

"Oh, how awful!" Jane's eyes were bright with tears. "But he did find him?"

"Yes. He found him just in time to save the horse's life.

For Brioso had run a long splinter of wood into his shoulder in his struggle to get out of the horse-box, and the wound had become poisoned. Ramiro told me that he drew out the splinter himself and opened the wound to drain it then and there while Brioso lay on the grass in the New Forest."

"But——" began Mrs. Fortune.

"I know what you're going to say, Meg." There was the ghost of a grin on Uncle Leslie's face for the first time. "Ramiro told me that Brioso had other wounds too—made by teeth and hooves. He had fought with another stallion—and like all good knights, had won his lady-love! She was waiting at a respectful distance for Brioso to get up again—there was no doubt about it!"

"Gosh, this is exciting!" said Jeremy. "That must have been Betsy Jane—Falla's dam! So Falla is a half-bred Arab!"

"But how did Ramiro get to know about Falla?" said Mrs. Fortune.

A shadow came over Uncle Leslie's face.

"That's the unhappy part of the story," he said. "You see, Ramiro was some months before he could get Brioso fit enough to work again; he missed all that circus season, and then had to live through the winter. It was during that time, when for the first time in his life he knew what it was to be short of money, that he fell in with the Mendoza brothers.

"One of them, Carlos, had been in England for many years working around racing stables. His record was none too clean—he had been dismissed after a suspected doping incident, though nothing could be proved. The other, Miguel, was . . . well, one could say he was a genius gone wrong. He had served an apprenticeship in the bull-ring, but the dedicated life of a first-class matador was too hard for him. He took up with horses—and he could have been outstanding as a trainer since he could do anything with them. But once again his character let him down—he was too indolent, too erratic to stick at anything long. He came over to England and went into partnership with his brother—doubtful horse-dealing mostly. Then they met Ramiro at this bad period of his career—and that is where the trouble started."

Uncle Leslie paused, and his eyes were rather bleak. "They knew of Ramiro's fame and something of his nature. They knew he would spend money while it was there with no thought of the future. And they took advantage of his temporary trouble to get him so indebted that all his earnings were mortgaged far ahead—to the Mendoza brothers! Mind you, they were cunning about it. Even Ramiro himself doesn't realise how they have bled him.

"But the accident had changed Brioso. As he grew older the wound in his shoulder seemed to become troublesome again, even though it appeared to have healed."

"I know about that!" put in Jane. "Where Daddy broke his wrist when he was a little boy—it aches now he's getting old. Rude something gets in it."

"She means rheumatism," said Jeremy scornfully.

"That what I said. I s'pose rude-matism gets in Brioso's bad shoulder too."

"You're perfectly right," said Uncle Leslie gravely. "And it meant that Brioso couldn't give of his best. And Carlos and Miguel Mendoza began to realise that their nice little source of income might dry up unless they could find another horse for Ramiro Toral."

Uncle Leslie came back to the table and sat down again. "Well, you can probably guess the rest," he said. "They knew it wouldn't be easy to find a thoroughbred Arab at a price within their pockets. They knew the story of Brioso's short stay in the New Forest. And they did a bit of inquiring on their own. They must have spotted Falla, and found out that she would be among those auctioned last October. They just hadn't quite the amount of cash to outbid me—and they knew they weren't well enough known for their cheque to be accepted, even if they had a bank account, which I doubt. After that they decided to see how Falla shaped, and since she so obviously was exceptional they made their plans to get hold of her, by hook or by crook!"

Uncle Leslie sat up straighter, his eyes blazing now.

"You can imagine that when I realised that Ramiro was calmly talking about his plans for training Falla, I pretty well blew my top! At least, I had to keep my temper in check a bit, because—well, because Ramiro for all his faults is a great man in his own way and somehow one just doesn't treat him like a pickpocket! But I did bring out every argument I could—and none too politely at that. I reckon if it hadn't been for my old friendship with his family he'd have had me thrown out! I told him that Falla wasn't for sale on any account—she was already in the best of hands."

"And he said: '*Children!*' " put in Jane, with an intonation of scorn on the word.

"Yes, he did," admitted Leslie. "He said that it was wicked to waste the great powers of such a horse on children. He could train her to execute movements that no other living horse could do—he would make her great and famous."

"I don't want Falla to be a great . . . circus horse!" suddenly wailed Jane.

"I didn't intend that she should be," said her uncle crisply. "And I told him so. I said he and his friends would have to look elsewhere. And then I said something that I hope was wise . . ."

"What?" said his listeners all together.

"I said that the English police took a poor view of theft."

"Well, that was right," interjected Mr. Fortune.

"Yes—but it wasn't the right thing to say to a proud Andalusian. I'm afraid it ended any chance of more discussion. He stood up and said in an icy tone: 'There is no question of theft. Ramiro Toral pays for what he takes. And already the arrangements have been made for the mare to be conveyed to me.'

"Then he stalked over to the door and held it open for me. I can tell you, I shot out of it with no more ceremony, because his words could mean only one thing. All I could think of was to get back here in time to stop them taking Falla."

Uncle Leslie put his head down into his hands and groaned. "But I wasn't in time—I wasn't in time!"

Jane went over and hugged him.

"Don't worry, Uncle Leslie. You were awfully clever to find out all that. I don't feel so bad now that I know that Falla will be with people who understand horses." Her lip trembled just a little bit. "I think your Mr. Ramiro sounds an interesting person—but he can't have our Falla! We will get her back soon, won't we?"

Uncle Leslie stood up.

"You'll get her back the very first moment I can arrange it," he promised. "I'm going back there straightaway—and I shall get the police on to it if necessary."

"Excuse *me*!" put in Mrs. Fortune promptly. "You've driven about three hundred miles since yesterday afternoon with no sleep. You're not going to rush back to Gloucestershire without a meal and some rest. Good gracious! Apart from the fact that you'd be a menace on the roads, how would the children get Falla back on their own if you had an accident?"

Uncle Leslie smiled and suddenly yawned.

"Dear sister Meg, you're right," he said. "I think it was arguing with Ramiro did it! What d'you think, you kids? Shall I have an hour or two's rest first?"

"Of course!" Jeremy and Jane spoke together, and Jeremy added: "We can come too when you go, can't we?"

"No!" Mr. Fortune put his foot down firmly. "These two brothers—Mendoza or whatever their name is—are dangerous chaps to my mind. They've already given Jeremy a shot of dope——"

"But they didn't *hurt* me—and they could have!" said Jeremy.

"That's not to say what they might do if they were really cornered!" said Mr. Fortune grimly. "Leslie, I forbid you to take them!"

"O.K., John, you're the boss," said Leslie. "Meg—if you'll give me a drink and a sandwich or something I'll doss down for a couple of hours before I go."

When their uncle was stretched out on his bed—he could drop off to sleep immediately at any time he wanted to—the two children wandered off down the lane. By common consent they turned away from the lane leading to the water meadow. Even though they knew that Falla was safe they could not bear to see her shed and field empty.

"Oh, J., I feel so lost without her!" whispered Jane.

"Shut up!" said Jeremy fiercely. "What d'you think I feel like?" He kicked at a stone gloomily. "Oh, bother, isn't it all horrible! There's this Spanish chap, upset because his wonderful horse is getting too old and wanting to turn Falla into a second Brioso."

"He can't! He can't take Falla—she's ours!" cried Jane.

"Of course he can't," agreed Jeremy. "But somehow, though I don't really want to, I feel a sort of sneaking sympathy. Well, not even that really—it's just that I can understand his point of view. It's a sort of crime to him not o bring out every ounce of performance that a horse is capable of. You can understand why he thinks it a waste for wo children to have Falla."

Jane stopped and pondered deeply. This took a lot of hinking over, and she gave it all her attention.

"Yes, I can see that too," she said slowly. "But—but think Falla's happier with us. She knows how much we ove her—I'm sure she does! And however wonderful she s, the training will be much harder than anything we vould give her."

"Gosh, I do wish we could go with Uncle Leslie and ee this Ramiro chap," said Jeremy, changing the subject.

"So do I," said Jane wistfully. "But Daddy wouldn't hear of it. You heard him forbid Uncle Leslie to take us."

Jeremy suddenly grinned.

"And Uncle Leslie wouldn't do it," he said.

"Of course he wouldn't. J.—what're you thinking about?"

"I was just thinking that it's no good saying to him: 'Uncle Leslie, can we come with you?' because he'd say 'No.' But supposing he didn't know we were there? Supposing we were stowed away in the back of his car and we popped up when he got to Gloucestershire! He couldn't get into trouble because he hadn't done anything and *Daddy didn't actually say to us 'Don't go!'* "

Jane stared at Jeremy with her mouth open. Then a wide grin spread over her face.

"Oh, J.—let's!" she said.

CHAPTER EIGHT

"THE BIRDS HAVE FLOWN"

UNCLE LESLIE's big old Lagonda was still parked outside the water meadow where he had left it that morning.

"The best place would be for us to lie on the floor at the back. There's plenty of room, and we can sort of drape that rug he keeps on the back seat over us."

"Hold on a minute!" said Jeremy, feeling Jane was rather rushing things. "We can't just go off like that. I've got to fix up my paper round for one thing. And for another—what are we going to say to Mum and Dad?"

"Couldn't—couldn't we ask for a picnic and say we're going out for the rest of the day?" she suggested. "That wouldn't really be a fib, would it."

"It'd be true," said Jeremy, then added: "As far as it went," because he was fundamentally honest and didn't like the thought of deceiving his parents.

Jane didn't like it either, and said so. "I know it's not right. But J., I can't just sit waiting for Uncle Leslie to bring Falla back. We'll tell Mummy and Daddy afterwards and take our punishment . . . but I must go!"

Jeremy sighed.

"That's how I feel about it too," he said. "And I don't think there's any more use talking. Come on, let's see if Porky Miller will do my round for me."

Porky was quite willing to take over for that evening, and Mrs. Fortune agreed to pack up sandwiches for them for the rest of the day. She even seemed rather pleased that they had found something to occupy them.

"You'll get back before dark, won't you?" she counselled them.

"What time's Uncle Leslie going?" asked Jane.

"He asked me to call him about one o'clock. He'll go as soon as he's had some lunch, I expect." Mrs. Fortune looked at Jane's face averted and added: "Don't worry, Janey. He'll get Falla back safely!"

By common consent the children chose a spot to eat their lunch where they could watch the car without being in view of Falla's empty shed. When they heard the church clock in the village strike one o'clock Jeremy rose to his feet with a sigh.

"We'd better be getting in," he said.

They found there was plenty of room for them to lie on the floor in the roomy old car. The backs of the front seats sloped, and they would be invisible where they lay unless someone knelt on a front seat and looked right over.

After a few preliminary wriggles they got comfortable, and it wasn't long before they heard Uncle Leslie's footsteps.

Afterwards Jeremy and Jane were to remember that ride as the most uncomfortable time in their lives. The floor of an old car with pre-war springing is not the place to lie full-length when the car is being driven fast on English roads. Hidden as they were they could not anticipate any movements of the car when it turned corners, and they were unmercifully bumped, biffed and shaken.

"I—c-can't stand much more of this!" gasped Jane under cover of the noise of the engine.

"You've got to!" said Jeremy through set teeth. He wedged himself with his feet. "We must have been going over an hour. Count up to five hundred slowly and then I think we can show ourselves, because he'll be too far from home to turn round and take us back."

They gritted their teeth and counted five hundred, then a hundred more to make sure.

"Here goes!" said Jeremy, beginning to push the rug back.

"Wait a minute!" Jane clutched him. "We're stopping!"

Sure enough, they had felt the car swing round to the right and travel along an extra bumpy track before coming to a halt. Before Jeremy could move, the front car door opened, then slammed again. Heaving his aching body up Jeremy was just in time to see the back of Uncle Leslie's head as he walked rapidly through a farm gate which swung to after him.

"Jane, we're there!" he cried, rubbing the sore places on his elbows. "Thank goodness for that!"

"Ow!" said Jane, struggling to her feet. "I've got pins and needles and *millions* of bruises!"

"Never mind that!" Jeremy was opening the door of the car. "Come on, Uncle Leslie went through that gate."

They couldn't start at once, because they had to wait for the feeling to come back into Jane's leg before she could walk.

"I wonder where Falla is?" she said, balancing on her good leg. "Can you see her in any of the fields round here, J.?"

Jeremy got up on to the bank at the side of the cart track and looked all round from this higher vantage point.

"Not a sign," he reported. "But I can see the farm buildings—she's probably in the stables there."

"Come on—hold my arm! I can't wait to see her again!" Jane clutched Jeremy's arm and they proceeded in a three-legged way as fast as they could through the gate.

There was no sign of their uncle as they turned the corner leading to the farmhouse. And—stranger still—there was no sign of anyone. The little farmhouse and the outbuildings were quiet and seemingly empty; no sound of chickens clucking or of the unmistakable sounds of a farm.

"That's funny," said Jeremy with a frown. "Shall I knock on the door?"

Jane stopped and looked round her. Then she shivered a little.

"No, don't knock," she said. "I—I don't like it here very much. I'm sure it shouldn't be as quiet as this."

"Well, we must do *something*," said Jeremy reasonably. He pointed over to the other side of the farmyard where there were some stable buildings. "Let's go and look over there."

There were two or three loose-boxes, and the divided doors were swinging half open. All the boxes were empty, though the children found signs that a horse had been there quite recently. In the manger were oats scattered as if they had been blown.

"I know Falla's been here!" declared Jane. "She always blows her feed like that, and then spends ages picking up each little bit separately . . ." her voice wobbled. "Oh, J. —where *is* she?"

"I think we'd better find Uncle Leslie first," said Jeremy. "He's sure to know what's happened."

They filed dejectedly out of the loose-box and over to the farmhouse again. When they approached the door they noticed that it was ajar, and on an impulse Jeremy pushed it open. After only a moment's hesitation he walked in, followed rather fearfully by Jane. They paused in the passageway and listened, but there was no sound. Then Jane called out in a rather quavery voice: "Uncle Leslie! Are you there?"

There was no reply, and the silence seemed to get thicker and thicker. Jane's face was very white, and she caught

hold of Jeremy's arm. "J., let's go back to the car! I don'
like it here!" she whispered.

Jeremy knew just how she felt. He too wanted to tur
tail, but just in time he remembered that he was thirtee
and nearly grown up.

"D-don't be silly, Janey," he said in a normal—or nearl
normal voice. "Hi!" he called, hoping he sounded brav
and nonchalant. "Hi! Hello! Anyone there?"

Even though there was still no sound his own voice ha
given him back some courage, for he turned back to Jan
and said boldly: "I'm going to look round—we migh
find a clue."

Without another word Jane followed him. They wen
into the downstairs rooms first, and found plenty of evidenc
of a hasty departure. Chairs were slewed round, rugs ha
skidded wildly out of place, scattered papers were every
where. Jeremy picked up one of them and opened i
out.

"It's a picture of Falla!" cried Jane, looking over hi
shoulder. "Oh, no, it isn't. That's a stallion, but . . .
know, J., it's Brioso . . . he *must* be Falla's sire! She'
just like him!"

The resemblance was plain, even without the captio
underneath. "RAMIRO TORAL WITH BRIOSO, HI
WORLD-FAMOUS DANCING ARAB HORSE." Th
horse was executing a half-rear, its beautiful strong nec
arched so that its crest stood up in a fierce line.

Jane voiced both their thoughts.

"I don't want Falla to be like that!" she said decisively
"It's very beautiful, but she's ours, not a performing horse!"

Jeremy pulled himself together with a start and stuffe
the leaflet into his pocket.

"We've got the upstairs to do," he said.

The stairs were rather dark, and when Jane's hand foun

his Jeremy was more relieved than otherwise. The two small rooms upstairs showed the same evidence of hasty withdrawal—drawers pulled out, and a general untidiness. But the children couldn't help noticing that there were no personal belongings left at all.

"I think they must have rented this cottage furnished with the stables, and done a bunk as soon as they got Falla," said Jeremy. "They might have gone anywhere—unless Uncle Leslie knows."

"But we don't even know where Uncle Leslie is!" suddenly wailed Jane.

"So it was you two I heard upstairs!" said a voice in the doorway, and the children whirled round to see their uncle standing there. He must have come in the door and up the stairs silently as a shadow. But the expression on his face wasn't the one they were used to; his blue eyes were icy and his mouth was grim.

"May I ask what you're doing here—when your parents expressly forbade you to come?" he said coldly.

The two children gazed at one another in dismay. This was awful—their kind, friendly uncle so cold and angry.

"I—they didn't exactly forbid us," it was Jeremy who found his voice first. "They only said you mustn't take us—and you didn't know you *were* taking us . . " his voice tailed away. The explanation sounded feeble even to himself.

Jane created a diversion by rushing over to her uncle, flinging her arms round him and bursting into tears. Jeremy just stared with his mouth open. Jane wasn't usually so badly upset.

"Uncle Leslie—we're sorry, really, and we know we'll get into trouble," she sobbed. "But I felt I couldn't bear to sit and sit waiting and not knowing what was happening! Don't be angry, please—it's all so awful . . . because Falla isn't here and I hate this place and I do *ache* so much after the back of your car."

"Hold on—that'll do!" Uncle Leslie's face had softened, and he took hold of Jane's shoulders and gave her a little shake. "All right—you know it was wrong, and we're all going to get into a row when we get back."

"You won't!" put in Jeremy. "Because you didn't know!"

"Meg'll say I should have searched the car first," he said ruefully. "You know what sisters are like, don't you, Jeremy!" He gave Jeremy a half grin and fished out a large handkerchief from his pocket, which he handed silently to Jane, talking nonchalantly as she hiccuped herself into silence. "But that can wait. The important thing is that the birds have flown—as I expect you know by now."

"I think Falla was here—they gave her a feed!" came Jane's muffled tones, and Jeremy explained about the oats blown round the manger.

"Yes—before packing her into their horse-box and taking her off," said Uncle Leslie. "Come on down, both of you, and I'll show you the trail as far as it goes."

He led the children out into the yard and up to the loose-box, and then reconstructed the departure for them. Jeremy could not help admiring the way he could state what had happened from the smallest clues—a shaped wedge of mud from a horse's hoof, faint footprints, leading to a churned-up piece of ground—"I should say Falla played up here a bit . . . there's another horse's print not far off. Probably Ramiro's stallion—I expect Falla started dancing when she heard him whinnying."

"That *is* Falla's hoofmark," stated Jane, on her hands and knees by a patch of mud. "Look—it's a very clear one, and you can see the nail marks—one's in a different hole, because Joe had to put in another nail when the other worked loose, remember?"

"You'll make a detective one day," said her uncle. "Jeremy, can you go on from there?"

Jeremy studied the ground.

"The horse-box was backed in here," he said slowly. "There are its tyre tracks, and the mark where the tailboard was lowered. Those are the footprints of the men when they fastened up the back again—and they're the same as the ones in the water meadow, or jolly like them."

"Yes, the two Mendozas were here, all right," Uncle Leslie nodded.

"Then they drove out, through this gate, which swings shut . . ."

"And as far as the main road, where they turned south. But of course there'll be no marks to track them after that," finished Uncle Leslie.

"What shall we do now?" asked Jane.

"I think we ought to tell the police!" interrupted Jeremy. "Don't you, Uncle? After all, they've stolen Falla. Well, I know they left some money, but they took her away without —without consent, or whatever it is."

Uncle Leslie didn't reply for a moment. His face was very thoughtful, and when he spoke his voice was almost hesitant.

"Perhaps we ought . . . but I'd very much sooner you didn't do that," he said quietly.

The children stared at him open-mouthed for a moment, then Jeremy said in a puzzled voice:

"Why, is there something you know about it—something different?"

Their uncle seemed to be searching for the right words before he spoke.

"Jeremy—both of you," he said at last. "I know just how you feel. Falla is yours. You want her back more than anything—and as far as that's concerned I haven't done much to help so far. If you want to go to the police I can't stop you, and if that's what you decide after you've heard me we'll go straight to the nearest police station. But—can I ask you to trust me a little longer? It's a lot to ask . . . but you see, I know Ramiro. He is a proud, difficult man—but not a bad one. He would never ill-treat Falla in any way—it's just not in his nature to be unkind to a horse. In his queer, twisted way he feels that Falla is his by right and I know he feels this so strongly that he has no sense of guilt, no sense that he has done wrong. Now, if we go to the police, two things could happen. Either he might get wind of what was happening and leave the country at once—in which case it might take months before we caught up with him; or they might catch him before he could escape, and you would have Falla back quickly . . ."

"But isn't that what we want?" Jane put in.

"Go on, Uncle Leslie. There's something more to it than that, isn't there?" said Jeremy quietly.

"Yes, there is," said his uncle. "You see—there's a criminal charge. Not only taking the horse, but drugging Jeremy too . . . it's quite serious. He'd probably get a prison sentence—and the Mendozas would, too."

"I think that's what they deserve," said Jane.

"Yes," admitted Uncle Leslie. "But—it would mean that he would be separated from Brioso, his horse. The relationship between those two is something quite extraordinary. As Brioso gets older his attachment to his master becomes stronger, and I know if he weren't able to see Ramiro he would just fade away. Even though his working life is nearing its end he is still Ramiro's faithful companion. The bond between a horse like that and his master is something we ordinary 'horsey' people find it hard to understand."

"I know," Jane nodded. "He'd feel even worse than we

do about being parted from Falla—much worse! But Uncle Leslie, we can't just let him keep her!"

"Of course not—I wouldn't suggest that!" said her uncle, putting his hand on her shoulder. "But—if you would be patient just a little longer, I will appeal once more to Ramiro and, you see, if it is no good, I will be able to make sure that he does not escape abroad in the last resort. Would you trust me a bit more?"

"We do trust you," said Jeremy. "You know we do."

"Would it take very long?" Jane's eyes were big.

"Look, we'll make a time limit," said her uncle. "Say a fortnight . . . if you haven't heard anything from me, you can tell the police."

"D'you think he'll be easily alarmed—I mean scoot off abroad at the least thing?" said Jeremy.

"No, I'm pretty sure that he'll stay in England if he possibly can; he's on a good line here for the circus season —and he needs the money. And I shall see that there's nothing done to alarm him!"

The two children looked at one another, then turned to their uncle.

"We'll leave it to you, then, please," Jane spoke for both of them.

Her uncle's hand tightened on her shoulder.

"I feel very honoured," he said soberly. "And I won't let you down." He glanced down at his watch. "But the first thing now is to get you two back home. What did you say to your mother about where you were going?"

"We asked for a picnic," muttered Jeremy shamefacedly.

"Mummy said to be back before dark," added Jane.

"Um—we might just about do it, then." Their uncle led the way towards the car again. "But you'll have to tell her where you've been, even if we are back in time."

"Yes, we must take our medicine," said Jeremy resignedly.

The ride home was more comfortable physically than the journey north had been, but it was silent nevertheless. All of them were preoccupied with their own thoughts.

It was growing darker as they came along the Heath road. A group of New Forest ponies which had been rolling in a swamp and were covered in black mud clattered across the road in front of them and cantered off across the scrub.

"Oh," said Jane in a small voice.

Jeremy and Uncle Leslie spoke together quickly in rather loud voices.

"It's not quite dark yet——"

"Lucky we didn't meet much traffic——"

They too had noticed that one of the ponies had a free, swinging canter that reminded them momentarily of Falla. In the small confusion the difficult moment passed, and Jane regained her self-control enough to add shakily: "Yes, we'll be home soon now."

At the end of their lane their uncle halted the car.

"D'you want me to come in and help you face the music?" he asked. "Or shall I go straight back and get on the trail?"

"Go back!" said the children together, though Jane remembered to add: "If you aren't too tired after all that driving."

"I'm not tired at all," their uncle assured them. "I'll catch up on sleep when the job's over! O.K., in you go! And if you haven't heard from me in a fortnight—straight to the police!" He paused then added grimly: "But if it comes to that—I shall hand Interpol my resignation on a soup plate!"

And he revved up his engine and shot off into the darkness.

CHAPTER NINE

A SECOND ARAB PONY?

When it came to the point, "facing the music" wasn't as bad as Jeremy had expected. Jane unwittingly saved the day. Exhausted by emotion and the battering they had had on the journey north, she distinguished herself by crumpling into a small unconscious heap on the kitchen floor as soon as they got indoors. By the time she had been put to bed and their mother was downstairs again Jeremy himself didn't feel too good. His mother took one look at his greenish face and packed him off to bed too without further delay.

In the morning they had to explain, of course, but in a way it was a relief to get it off their chests. They both felt decidedly achey and tired and their parents' decree that they must stay in for the rest of the day did not come at all as an arduous punishment.

The following day was Sunday, and they both woke up feeling better.

"School to-morrow," said Jane as they wandered into the garden after breakfast.

"D'you know—I'm rather glad," said Jeremy. "It'll sort of take our minds off things."

"Let's go up and see Mr. Hutchinson," said Jane. "There's always something going on at a farm."

Jeremy thought that was a good idea, and they set off for Brockenhurst Farm. Suddenly Jane stopped.

"Shall we tell him about Falla?" she asked.

Jeremy considered.

"We don't want it to get around," he said slowly. "But if he asks we'll have to let him know, because he's been so decent to us. We'll just tell him and swear him to deadly secrecy."

But as it turned out they didn't need to, because all Mr. Hutchinson said was:

"That mare o' yours all right? I reckon she's still up to Miss Long, being as I haven't seen her in the meadow lately."

The children made non-committal noises, glad not to have to explain, and the farmer went on:

"I'm proper glad to see you both, though. Would you be able to give a bit of a hand? I've some new calves wanting a home, and the old shed, she's full o' junk. I'd be grateful to have it cleared out."

"Of course, we'll like doing that!" cried Jane.

The two children set to work with a will, hauling out all the bits of scrap iron and making a heap of them by the fence near the road for the local scrap merchant to collect.

"Gosh!" panted Jeremy, wiping a dirty hand over his hot face. "I shouldn't think Mr. Hutchinson has ever thrown anything away in his life! Look at this—blow me if it isn't an ancient old bicycle, or part of it anyway!"

He tugged at a rusty piece of iron that stuck out from underneath a pile of papers. It wouldn't move, so Jane joined him. Suddenly it came free with a rush, and the two children fell flat on their backs while a huge pile of newspapers cascaded down like giant snowflakes.

"Help!" gasped Jane. Jeremy struggled to his feet, shedding newspapers in all directions, and fished under the pile for Jane. He grasped the hand he could see sticking out and hauled on it vigorously.

At that moment Mrs. Hutchinson issued from the farmhouse door with two long glasses of orangeade and some cakes on a tray.

"My goodness, you've got a job and a half there!" she chuckled. "Here's something to wash the dust down—and some of my home-made gingerbread too."

"Oh, thank you, Mrs. Hutchinson. We're really rather enjoying it," Jeremy assured her.

When she returned to the house they sat down on the heap of newspapers to eat their gingerbread. Jane idly picked up one of the papers and began to look through it.

"It's an old local paper," she said. "The kind you deliver weekly." She turned over a page. "New Forest Notes—by Sag—Sagittarius," she read out carefully. "That's a funny name."

"It's quite a good name," Jeremy said. "It means an archer in Latin, and William Rufus was shot by an arrow in the New Forest . . . New Forest Notes . . . it's clever, really."

But Jane wasn't listening. She was reading through the short paragraphs that made up the column.

"An unusual and interesting sight met these poor old eyes to-day," she read out. "A sturdy little pony—one of our New Forest matrons . . . *matrons?* What on earth does he mean?"

"He means one of the mares I expect," Jeremy was rather bored.

". . . matrons, with—with—*Jeremy!* listen to this! 'With twin grey foals at her heels!' "

"Twin grey . . . what date's that paper?" Jeremy was alert at once. He scrambled over and seized it from her. "Nearly three years ago!" They stared at each other with round eyes for a moment, then Jeremy read on:

"And what is more, gentle readers, every line of their delicate legs and dainty heads showed breeding. These were not our usual English stock. Has a Prince Charming visited these New Forest lands?"

"Ugh!" Jeremy summed up their dislike of this sugary prose.

"Jeremy, one of them could have been Falla!" Jane was hopping round in excitement. "She may be a twin! Does it say any more?"

"It says one was a colt and one a filly—at least, he says a boy and a girl, but that's what he means," said Jeremy scornfully.

"Falla's got a brother—I just know it!" breathed Jane. "I wish we could tell Uncle Leslie."

"We can't until we get an address to write to," said Jeremy, gloomy again. "Anyway, it doesn't help us."

But Jane was obviously boiling over with some idea.

"It doesn't help *us*—but perhaps it would help Mr. Ramiro! J., wouldn't it be lovely if he could have the other grey, when we get Falla back?"

"Um." Jeremy wasn't as tender-hearted as Jane, and he didn't think Ramiro deserved such consideration, but he turned over in his mind what Jane had said.

"The only thing is," he pointed out. "This grey would be the same age as Falla, and it's not very likely that he hasn't been rounded up for sale by now."

"I think it *is* likely," said Jane stoutly. "You know how stallions lead a little bunch of mares away and go quite wild and difficult to catch. Anyway," she finished. "We must tell Uncle Leslie."

When the shed was clear they stayed to enjoy the enormous bonfire which burnt up all the burnable rubbish. Jeremy tore out the "Sagittarius" article and stuffed it into the pocket of his jeans.

They arrived home, dirty but reasonably content, in time for lunch, which was at two o'clock on Sundays. They were just clearing up their second helpings of pudding when there was an official-sounding rat-tat on the front door.

"I'll go!" said Jeremy scrambling for the door before Jane could forestall him.

On the doorstep was the son of the postmaster, who did telegraph-boy duty over the week-ends.

"Telegram for yer Mum," he said, handing it to Jeremy. "I got to wait in case there's an answer, see."

Jeremy handed over the orange envelope to his mother. She opened it with a worried frown—telegrams were quite a rarity in the Fortune family and were liable to bring news of illness. Then her brow cleared.

"Oh, it's from Leslie," she said. "Tell Jimmy there's no reply, will you dear?"

Jeremy obeyed, as Jane burst out:

"Is there any message for us, Mummy?"

"You'd better read it—it's mostly for you, though he has the grace to apologise to me," Mrs. Fortune added severely.

Jeremy and Jane were reading the telegram together. It said:

"Sorry, Meg. Tell kids trail is warm. Chins up. Any letters c/o P.O. Box 17, Nailsworth."

"Nailsworth—I saw signposts saying that near that farm," said Jeremy. "Good—we can write to Uncle Leslie now."

"Let's do it this afternoon," said Jane. "We—we can tell him our chins *are* up!"

"O.K.," agreed Jeremy. Obviously Jane wanted to keep the newspaper cutting a secret until they had told Uncle Leslie.

However, after dinner they found they weren't able to get down to writing to Uncle Leslie at once. They had both forgotten all about their week-end homework in all the excitement of the last few days, and Mr. and Mrs.

Fortune took a stern line about it, insisting that they do it straight away, in spite of their protests that the evening would do.

Then when they did start the letter, about four o'clock, it didn't go as quickly as it might have done, because Jane wanted to put in about letting Ramiro have the other grey instead of Falla, and Jeremy told her it was a silly idea and just like a girl to dream up something that was probably impossible. Quite a quarrel developed, and they were both glaring at each other when their mother came into the room.

"It's nearly six o'clock," she said. "Have you two finished? I want to lay the table."

"Golly—the Sunday post goes at six!" gasped Jeremy. He finished the sentence he was writing, added "Love" and his signature and pushed it over to Jane, who signed her name with her lower lip stuck out mutinously.

"Come with me to post it?" Jeremy offered.

"No thanks, you go on your bike. I'm tired," she said.

He stifled a sigh. "O.K.—I'll go. And Uncle Leslie will probably get it to-morrow morning."

Jane cycled with Jeremy on his paper round after school the next day and when it was finished they were ambling home when there was a sudden outburst of hooting behind them.

They glanced round and Jeremy gave a yell of delight.

"It's Uncle Leslie!" he shouted.

Jane had already flung her bicycle into the hedge and had scrambled into the other front seat of the car.

"Have you had our letter? How's Falla? D'you know where she is? Is she all right?" she bombarded her uncle with eager questions.

"One at a time!" he smiled. "Yes, she's all right. And I know where she is—though Ramiro doesn't know that

: know! She's quite safe and well. Come on, let's get in-
loors and I'll tell you all the news."

Jeremy and Jane waited with what patience they could
intil their uncle was indoors and seated in an arm-chair
vith his legs stretched out.

"Go on, tell us all that's happened!" Jane demanded.

"Well," their uncle began. "It wasn't hard to trace
Ramiro. In fact, he's only about twenty miles away from
he farm where we were, but he's lying pretty low until he
ıas Falla trained. I got in touch with Landers, the circus
ooss, but for some reason he wasn't very oncoming. I
hink Ramiro's been playing up a bit. He just told me
ather shortly that Ramiro hadn't given him a date when
ıe might join the circus yet."

"But when's she coming back?" asked Jane. "It seems
uch ages . . ."

Uncle Leslie reached out a gentle hand and pulled one of
ane's plaits.

"I know," he said soberly. "Trust me a bit longer.
want to talk about your letter—and why it was so impor-
ant. You've gathered by now that it's going to be very
lifficult to get Ramiro to part with Falla without a lot of
ınpleasantness. Though if you give the word I'd get her
ack here to-morrow . . ."

The two children looked at one another and Jeremy spoke
or both of them.

"We can wait," he said quietly. "As long as you say so,
Jncle Leslie."

"But I think I can see a solution here, in this cutting.
The dates are right. It looks as though Brioso sired two
reys——"

"And Ramiro could have the other one!" squeaked Jane.
'I said so! Didn't I, Jeremy? Isn't that what I said? I told
ou! Uncle Leslie—I told him . . .!"

"Here, steady on!" pleaded their uncle. "Don't blow your top, Janey. All right, I think it'd be a good idea too. But we've got to find him first—set about tracing his owner, or find out whether he has been rounded up for sale yet. What are the chances of his being still at large, d'you think?"

"Jane thinks he probably is," said Jeremy, a little shaken by his uncle's ready acceptance of what he had considered a far-fetched idea. "We'd have to find out his owner——"

"Oh, you are silly!" Jane was hopping with exasperation. "I know where to find *that*! His name'll be on your catalogue—the one you had at the Sale. The man who owns Falla's dam—he'll be the owner of the other grey as well!"

Jeremy stared at Jane with unwilling admiration.

"It's an idea," he said. "Just a minute—I know where the catalogue is."

He fetched it from his bedroom and they turned up the entry.

"J. Fildred, Winchester. Crumbs, that's not much," he said disappointedly.

"It's enough," said his uncle decidedly. "I'll look in the phone book first—and I can get in touch with the auctioneers if that's no good. They'll have his particulars." He rose to his feet and stretched. "O.K.—that's the plan," he said. "Find the owner, trace the horse, see if he's for sale—then a fair exchange with Falla. Otherwise——"

"Otherwise we'll have to have Falla back anyway," said Jeremy stubbornly.

"But I would like Ramiro to have another Arab," said Jane thoughtfully. "I—somehow I understand how he feels."

They all trooped down to the telephone box to make a start on the plan, but at first they drew a blank. There was no Fildred on the telephone in the Winchester area, nor could Directory Inquiry trace one.

The firm of auctioneers was more helpful. They looked

up their records and gave the address of Mr. Fildred—though adding that he travelled round the country a good deal.

"Well," said their uncle as they came out. "That's all we can do for now. To-morrow I'll be off early to find this chap."

Their uncle had gone when they got up the next morning, and when it came to the end of the day they both raced home from school, hoping for some news. But there was nothing, and they had to be as patient as they could until the next morning.

Jeremy was downstairs waiting for the postman when the letter came and he hastily tore the envelope open and unfolded the single sheet of paper.

Fildred is in Scotland. Am going there straight away. No record of grey being sold at Beaulieu Road auctions. Will write again soon as I can. L.

"No record of sale at auction," said Jeremy thoughtfully. "That could mean that he's still free. Or he might have been privately sold . . . though that's not so likely as Falla was up for auction."

"D'you know what I think we ought to do," said Jane. "Go exploring through the forest to see if we can spot the grey anywhere."

"Don't be silly," said Jeremy. "There are hundreds of miles of New Forest." He thought it over, then changed his mind. "I dunno, though—it's worth trying. We might just be lucky."

But they were frustrated in this plan, for that day and the next it rained so hard that their mother put her foot down and forbade them to go out again after Jeremy had returned from his paper round drenched to the skin.

But on the Friday the weather cleared, and a day of warm sunshine dried out the ground. That evening, as soon as

Jeremy had finished his paper round, they got out their bicycles and climbed up the hill to where the Heath road stretched across the New Forest scrub land.

They could see groups of ponies in the distance, but none of them contained a grey. In fact the only item of any interest was a sack of rolled oats which lay by the side of the road. It had obviously fallen from the top of an overloaded lorry, for it had split its fastening in the fall and was spilling out and blowing in all directions.

"We'd better pick it up," said Jeremy. "The ponies will make themselves ill if they find this. You remember that roan pony, Copper, who got at the feed-bin?"

Jane shuddered. "Yes—he gorged and gorged and nearly died of colic," she said.

They gathered up what they could into the sack and Jeremy tied it with the string that had been round the neck of the sack.

Jeremy hoisted the sack on to his handlebars and they cycled home, feeling rather flat, even though they hadn't expected much.

"We'll try again to-morrow," said Jane stoutly.

That night the wind dropped and the weather turned hot and close. Jeremy could not sleep.

He got up and padded over to the window. Everything was silver and black, and the air was delicious outside. The sky was clear, except for that ominous bank of clouds which was still quite low in the east.

Jeremy looked from his stuffy bedroom to the coolness outside, and made up his mind. He slipped on his jeans and a shirt, and picking up his plimsolls tiptoed to the door. But before he could open it, it was pushed open from the other side, and a small figure in pyjamas confronted him.

"You're going out! Wait for me—I'm coming too!" Jane whispered.

Jeremy opened his mouth to protest, then shut it again. He knew it was no good when Jane's mind was made up.

Jane was ready in roughly twenty seconds, and they slipped silently out of the back door. By common consent they took the slope up to the Heath road.

"We'll just go up there and back," said Jeremy.

The bank of cloud in the east was a little higher now, and had thrown out a few outriders. One of these drifted across the face of the moon as they reached the beginning of the Heath road, but there was still a faint light to see by.

Suddenly Jeremy stopped and gripped Jane's arm. "Look!" he breathed.

Where the scattered oats had fallen there was a group of New Forest ponies busily gathering up the last of what was left. One of them was blowing softly through his nose as he searched for the odd bits among the grass.

"That's what Falla does!" whispered Jane in Jeremy's ear. Faint though the sound was the ponies heard it, and their heads jerked up.

Both the children froze in their tracks, and for a moment nothing moved. The horses stood like statues, their heads raised and turned towards the sound they had heard.

Then the moon sailed triumphantly out of the cloud and bathed the scene in brilliant silver light. Jeremy heard Jane catch her breath sharply, and his own heart gave a great thump.

For the foremost horse—the leader of the little group—gleamed grey in the moonlight, and they could see that he had the unmistakable small, elegant head and short back that showed Arab blood.

CHAPTER TEN

MIDNIGHT CAPTURE

For a long moment it seemed as if nothing would ever move again. Then, from the menacing bank of cloud, came a low rumble of thunder, and at the sound the spell was broken. The small band of ponies tossed their heads and moved uneasily, seemingly undecided whether to stay and search for more oats or make off. But the grey was obviously the leader, for he came forward a short step, and then stopped, his beautiful head with pricked ears turned towards the children.

Jeremy reached out a cautious hand to put on Jane's arm where she stood beside him, and then his blood ran cold—for she wasn't there!

Then he saw a movement, and the next moment she had stepped out of the shade into the brilliant moonlight, and was advancing towards the grey, her hand stretched out, crooning to him gently.

Jeremy clenched his hands.

Oh help! he thought. It might be dangerous . . . he's defending his band—he might attack her! He tried to call out, but no sound would come. His throat felt as if it had dried up.

The grey snorted and retreated a step before Jane's advance. The ponies behind him were bunched together, ears twitching uneasily.

There was a flash of lightning from the cloud behind them, followed by an ominous crack of thunder as the dark nass crept up the sky to overtake the moon. And, as if riggered off by the sound, chaos broke loose.

The grey stallion flung up his head with a shrill whinny, ınd the bunch of ponies wheeled and galloped away, manes ınd tails flying. The grey, too, half reared as he turned to follow them.

Then Jeremy could hardly believe his eyes, for the grey lid not complete his movement of flight. He dropped his orefeet to the ground again, and was staring at Jane, ears cocked, his whole aspect no longer menacing but interested.

Jane was standing without moving, and she was making ıer chirruping sound to the grey horse. But it was not quite he same noise—it had a shriller, more urgent note in t.

And the grey was moving now. The awe-struck Jeremy aw him take a hesitant step forward, then another . . . ınd another . . . until his proud head was bending to Jane's outstretched hand.

She moved closer then, and let her hand slip up to his ıeck. Now she was talking to him quietly, and he was tanding still, arching his neck to her stroking hand.

Without altering her quiet tone Jane said:

"Jeremy, can I have your belt? Come over here now—ıe's not frightened any more."

Jeremy let out a long breath, realising that he had been ıolding it for ages. He unbuckled the belt around his jeans—ıe only wore it to hold the sheath for his scout knife anyway—and holding it in one hand walked quietly out of the hadow and up to Jane and the grey horse.

The grey lifted his head as Jeremy came into the moonight, but Jane soothed him with a quiet word. Jeremy ıanded her the belt and she looped it round the horse's ıeck, holding the two ends in her hand.

"He'll follow us now," she said confidently. "He's very gentle really—just like Falla."

Jeremy felt the situation was getting rather out of hand. "Wh-where are you taking him?" he demanded.

"To our water meadow," Jane told him calmly. "There's shelter there if he wants it—and he won't be able to get out."

She set off down the Heath road towards home, the stallion stepping easily beside her. Jeremy followed dazedly, his head in a whirl. He felt he ought to be exerting his elder-brotherly authority somewhere, but he just didn't know where to start.

Another flash of lightning made him glance apprehensively at the sky. The moon was losing the race with the cloud now—it would be only a matter of minutes before the storm was on them.

"We'd better hurry," he said.

The door of the shed was still open. Jeremy had not had the heart or inclination to mend the padlock since Falla had gone. Jane encouraged the grey stallion to step into the shed, and he followed her docilely. There was still hay in the haynet, and Jane put in a handful of oats in the manger. "To keep him happy till we've gone," she said. Meanwhile Jeremy wedged the door open so that the horse could go in or out as he wished, and finally Jane slipped the belt off the animal's neck.

He was happily occupied blowing the oats and then muzzling round for them, exactly as Falla always did, and the two children slipped quietly out of the shed and over to the gate, which they shut and fastened firmly behind them.

At that moment the clouds at last caught up with the moon. There was another flash of lightning, and right on top of it a really deafening crack of thunder.

"We must get a move on home," said Jeremy, "or we'll e properly caught in it. Jane! Janey! What's the matter?"

For Jane was sitting on the ground, her head bent over er knees. Jeremy dropped down beside her.

"J., I feel awfully queer . . ." her voice was the merest hread. "I—I can't get up."

Jeremy took hold of her hand. It lay inert in his, cold nd clammy. He glanced up at the now inky sky—and nxiety made him speak sharply.

"You've got to!" he said. "Here—come on, I'll carry ou. Get your arms hooked round my neck. I'll take you n my back!"

For all her slight build Jane was not that much smaller han he was, and her dead weight was very near the limit f what Jeremy could carry. Before he had gone far his eart was thumping and he longed to stop to get his breath ack. But a heavy drop of rain which fell on his nose changed is mind, and he broke into a clumsy run.

He only just made it. Just as Jeremy reached their back oor and flung himself inside, the heavens opened and the ain fell in a solid sheet of water.

Another flash of lightning lit up the kitchen as Jeremy taggered over to the sofa and decanted Jane on to it. Then e collapsed across her feet, gasping for breath. After a hile he stood up, and by the next flash of lightning he saw hat Jane was sitting up and taking notice again.

"D'you feel all right to walk upstairs?" he whispered. or answer Jane stood up, and holding hands the two childen crept up the stairs. Jeremy helped Jane take off her hoes, though she did not bother to undress. She just umbled into bed as she was, and fell asleep before she could nswer Jeremy's good night.

Jeremy himself had intended to stay awake and think hings over, but suddenly everything was too much effort.

He just managed to get into his pyjamas and between the sheets before he too was fast asleep.

It seemed to him that he had been asleep only for five minutes before he was woken up by his mother shaking him.

"Goodness, you're a couple of sleepyheads this morning!" she said. "Nine o'clock—and neither of you up yet! Did the storm keep you awake?"

"N-no," said Jeremy truthfully. Then, as full remembrance came back to him, he said apprehensively "Have you called Jane yet?"

"I'm just going to."

Jeremy hastily swung his legs over the edge of the bed "I'll go, Mum," he offered. He had remembered that Jane wasn't even undressed. It would be bound to lead to awkward questions.

Jeremy went in to his sister. As he thought, she was still fast asleep dressed in her jeans and a jersey. He shook her vigorously. "Come on, wake up, Jane!" he implored.

She rolled over and opened one eye. Then she sat up and looked at him solemnly.

"Hallo, J.," she said with a yawn. "I've had such a funny dream."

"Never mind about dreams now. Get up, and don't let Mummy see that you've been to bed with your clothes on!"

Jane stopped yawning and regarded herself with a puzzled frown.

"What's happened? Why haven't I got my pyjamas on?" she asked.

"Jane!" Jeremy wanted to shake her. "Don't you remember—last night—the grey stallion—we put him in the water meadow?"

Jane was staring at him open-mouthed.

"But that was my dream!" she said. "D'you mean to say it's really happened?"

"Come on—you're not properly awake!" said Jeremy rather crossly. Then, remembering that she had been pretty groggy last night, he added with more kindness: "Go and slosh your head with cold water, and you'll feel better."

By the time Jane appeared downstairs for breakfast she was a little pale, but otherwise seemed quite herself again, judging by the enormous wink she gave Jeremy.

They ate their breakfast as quickly as they could without attracting undue notice, and slipped out of the house. The air after the storm was cool and fresh, and their spirits rose in the sparkling sunshine.

When they reached the water meadow the grey stallion was contentedly cropping the sweet grass near the hedge, and he raised his head and whinnied as they approached. He trotted straight over to Jane as if he had known her all his life.

"He's friendly already," Jane said in an awe-struck voice.

The horse followed them into the shed perfectly happily, and after cautiously experimenting with the body brush they set about grooming him.

"He really is handsome," said Jeremy at last. "Can't you imagine what he'll look like in a few weeks' time when the grass-fat is worked off him and he's really muscled up!"

"I know Ramiro will take him," declared Jane. Then, suddenly doubtful. "I suppose he couldn't possibly be already promised to anyone, could he?"

Jeremy did not answer immediately. He felt the hair on the horse's quarters carefully, and then examined the saddle patch, finishing by picking up the unshod hooves one by one.

"I don't think he's ever been handled at all," he said slowly. "There's no owner's brand—Falla had 'FD' you remember—anywhere on him. And there have never been any shoes on those feet—they're just worn naturally. I bet he's never let anyone get near him before you collared him last night. It must have been that funny sort of noise you were making."

"I don't remember any of it very well," confessed Jane. "I thought it was just my usual horse noise."

The grey seemed perfectly resigned to his captivity, even friendly, especially towards Jane. After some discussion they agreed to name him Storm for the time being—remembering how he had been caught to the accompaniment of thunder and lightning.

"Ramiro will give him a proper name," said Jane confidently. Jeremy nodded, but crossed his fingers for luck at the same time.

They set off home at lunch-time. Jeremy gave a whoop as they came into sight of their gate, for the familiar black Lagonda was parked outside. But just before they went in Jane grabbed Jeremy's arm.

"Don't tell Uncle Leslie anything till I say!" she begged in a whisper. "I want to—please, J."

Jeremy nodded. After all, Jane had been the one who had caught Storm—it was only fair that she should do as she liked about it.

Over lunch their uncle told them what he had been doing all the week.

"I did have a bit of a job finding our friend Fildred," he admitted. "He goes all over the British Isles. When I did finally catch him—in North Wales, actually—he sent me straight back to Lyndhurst with a letter to his agent who does all the horse-selling business for him. But once I'd got hold of the agent it was pretty plain sailing. He looked up all the records, and confirmed that there had actually been twin grey foals three years ago, dam Betsy ane, sire unknown. They both dodged being rounded ıp until last year when the filly—that's your Falla—was :aught and sold at Beaulieu Road. The colt was wily, and hey didn't ever manage to catch him. He has been several imes seen in the distance, but doesn't usually get near nough to people—in fact he's never been seen near a oad in day-time."

Jeremy caught Jane's eye for a brief moment, but she ;ave the smallest shake of her head, and he said nothing.

"But one thing's positive, at any rate. Fildred is perfectly villing to sell—provided we can catch the horse! And both ıe and the agent warned me that it would be no easy task!"

Jane finished her last mouthful and slipped from her chair.

"If you've had enough lunch, Uncle Leslie," she said vith unnatural politeness, "could you come out for a walk vith Jeremy and me? We've got a friend we'd like you to neet."

"I shall be delighted," he said gravely. "Your friend peaks English, I trust?"

"He—he's got rather a hoarse voice," said Jeremy uddenly, inspired, and both the children collapsed into ıelpless giggles.

The two children dragged their uncle at a brisk trot lown the lane, ignoring his protests that his lunch was being haken up.

"There!" they said together, pausing at the gate of the vater meadow.

Storm raised his lovely head from the grass and whickered . friendly greeting as he saw Jane.

"You see—I said he had a 'horse' voice!" crowed Jeremy.

CHAPTER ELEVEN

AT THE CIRCUS

JEREMY AND Jane had certainly succeeded in giving their uncle the surprise of his life. They had never seen him so completely taken aback. He just gazed from them to the horse and back again with his mouth open, and seemed to be lost for words.

Finally he said in a rather weak voice:

"Do—you—mean—to—tell—me—that—that you two just caught him on your own?"

"Well, it was Jane really," explained Jeremy. He told the story of their excursion last night, finishing: "Only we haven't told Mum and Dad, just in case they were shirty about our going out."

"It was so hot we couldn't sleep," explained Jane. "He was awfully easy to catch, though. I should think," she went on seriously, "he likes being talked to and treated as a person, not rounded up in a herd with men shouting at him."

Uncle Leslie scratched his head.

"Well—it beats me!" he said at length. "Are you sure this is the right horse? I mean, Brioso's offspring?"

"Pretty sure," said Jeremy. "It all fits in. His teeth show the same age as Falla."

"And he's like her in nature as well as looks," said Jane.

"And I've just remembered something." Jeremy was pulling a miscellaneous assortment out of the pocket of his jeans. "We've got a picture of Brioso—we picked it up at that farm last week." He sorted out the toffee papers and bus tickets and put them carefully back into his pocket, leaving a folded sheet which he handed to his uncle.

Uncle Leslie opened it and studied the leaflet closely.

"There's certainly a strong likeness," he said. "I shouldn't think there's any doubt that this is the sire of the horse you've got here."

"We're calling him Storm, just for the time being," Jane told him. She held out her hand for the leaflet and looked at the picture. "Isn't he exactly like Brioso—except that he's still grey of course. You might have picked a better copy, J. There were lots there, and this one's all bumpy."

"You mean crumpled," said Jeremy.

"No, I don't—I mean bumpy. Look, there are lines all sort of criss-cross on the picture."

Uncle Leslie had gone into the field and was making friends with Storm. Jeremy paused before following him and took back the leaflet. He looked at it carefully, then he gave a whistle.

"You know what the lines are," he said. "They're writing! Something was written on a piece of paper resting on a pile of these leaflets, and the writing came through." He held the paper up to the light and twisted it about, then added disappointedly, "But it's too faint to see what it is."

"It sticks out more on the back," said Jane.

Jeremy turned the paper over. "Yes," he said. "But it's the wrong way round like that."

"What's the wrong way round?" Their uncle returned to join in the conversation, and Jeremy explained and handed over the leaflet again.

"Hm!" said Uncle Leslie after a minute. "Hm. This might be interesting—but we'll need a mirror to read it properly. Let's go back home and see what it says."

In the sitting-room at home they held the paper up to the mirror, and after a bit of manœuvring were able to decipher some words which now appeared in raised writing.

"Write this down, Jeremy. I'll have to spell it out as it comes," said Uncle Leslie, and read out slowly:

"S A B A D O . . . then I can't read the next word, but there's a figure '17' after that."

"Go on!" said Jeremy impatiently. "What comes next?"

"It's a muddle after that," said their uncle. "I should think another letter was written on top of a note of something. But there's a little bit of the letter that comes clear at the end. S O—then a gap—H—gap—E A. Then there's a signature quite distinct—Ramiro Toral!"

Jeremy looked at what he had written down.

"It's not much," he said rather glumly. He had:

SABADO — — — 17 — — — SO . . . H . . . EA. RAMIRO TORAL.

"What's the first word mean?" asked Jane, then suddenly gave a squeak. "I know—it's Spanish!"

"Very brilliant!" said Jeremy sarcastically. "Considering where we found it and who it belonged to."

Jane looked crestfallen, and Uncle Leslie put in quickly: "It is Spanish, of course. It means 'Saturday'. It looks to me rather as if it was a date jotted down," he pulled out a pocket diary and consulted it. "Yes. There is Saturday the 17th of July. That fits in."

"It's next Saturday!" said Jeremy.

Jane had got a bit bored with the subject and was examining the rest of the room in the mirror.

"That's funny—the clock says a quarter to eight in the mirror, when really it's a quarter past four," she said.

"Quarter past four!" Jeremy shot out of his chair. "Golly, my paper round! See you later, Uncle Leslie!"

He did his round in record time, and as usual saved the last paper for his parents. When he came back into the house he found only his mother there.

As soon as Jeremy saw her he knew that the story of their night adventure had come out. He bowed his head meekly to the storm. Luckily his mother didn't know that Jane had nearly collapsed afterwards—even Jane herself didn't seem to remember that very clearly, as Jeremy knew.

"Sorry, Mum," he said, "I really am." Then, cheering up a little: "But we've got that lovely horse—have you seen him yet?"

His mother sighed resignedly.

"Horses—that's all you two think of. And Leslie's as bad!" she said. "Yes, the horse is a beauty all right. I've just been down to see him and Jane and Leslie are still there." She glanced at the clock on the mantelpiece. "Look, dear, I've got to go and see old Mrs. Francis. Get the tea ready, will you? They'll be back in a minute. I won't be long."

Jeremy, anxious to please and grateful at being let off so lightly, nodded, and had bread and butter cut and the table laid in no time. He filled the kettle, and while he waited for it to boil he picked up the paper he had brought in and glanced through it idly.

Then suddenly he stiffened and stared at the middle page, comprehension dawning on his face.

Jane and her uncle, strolling contentedly back from communing with Storm, were suddenly greeted by the sight of a whirling dervish, waving a paper in the air and scattering other sheets of it as he came, and yammering at about five hundred words a minute!

"It's here—July the 17th—this is what was on it—look, Uncle Leslie! There it is, right across the middle page! Landers' Mammoth Circus—week beginning Saturday 17th July, on Southsea Common. SOUTHSEA!" he finished triumphantly.

Leslie took the paper from Jeremy's shaking hand and

read it. Jane, infected by her brother's excitement, was adding her squeak to the general uproar.

"It was in the letter! Ramiro was writing to say that's when he's going to be with the circus——"

"Southsea was the word we couldn't read——"

Jeremy glanced at his uncle's face and suddenly stopped, looking a little sheepish.

"D'you think we're assuming too much?" he asked.

"No, no, on the whole it seems quite likely," said their uncle slowly. "It just struck me that it's a bit queer Landers didn't mention it when I spoke to him on the phone yesterday. He said a bit brusquely that nothing was definite yet, and rang off. But he must have had the letter from Ramiro—if we're right about it—and have known that he's opening at Southsea."

Jeremy looked rather crestfallen, then he brightened up a little.

"Couldn't we get hold of a programme or something about the circus in advance? That would say if Ramiro was going to be in it."

"There's a lot of smoke coming out of the kitchen!" interrupted Jane suddenly.

"Gosh, it's steam! I left the kettle on!" Jeremy rushed back into the house.

By the time he and Jane had followed Jeremy in, Uncle Leslie seemed to have come to a decision.

"How'd you two like a trip to Southsea to-morrow?" he said. "The advance agents of the circus usually go down the week before and plaster the town with posters. We'll see what we can find."

The next morning the two children piled into the Lagonda. "It'll only take about an hour to get there," said Uncle Leslie. "Bit more comfortable than your other ride, eh?"

They knew from the newspaper that the circus was to be

held on Southsea Common, but of course when they got there there was no sign of it. Nor could they find any posters.

"I expect we're too early—the town will probably be full of them to-morrow," sighed Jeremy.

They stopped at a cheerful, crowded coffee stall on the sea front for some Coca-Cola and hot dogs. The proprietor, a small fat man wearing a shirt, dazzlingly-patterned like a sunset, grinned at Jeremy.

"You stayin' for the circus next week-end?" he asked.

"Not staying, exactly. Why—d'you know something about it?" Uncle Leslie answered for Jeremy.

"Know something abaht it—bless yer, I worked in it for twenty years! Yer wouldn't think it ter look at me, but I was in the cowboy act—rough riding, rodeo stuff. Wasn't nothing I couldn't do on 'orseback—we 'ad a Wild West act that was really somethink!"

"D'you still keep in touch with the show?" asked Leslie.

"You bet I do—and I can tell yer——" the tubby little man hitched his stomach over the counter and leant forward confidentially. "I can tell yer it's a wunnerful show this year!"

"Who's in it?" asked Uncle Leslie.

"There's the Flying Foxes—trapeze, y'know. Boldero and 'is mixed lions and bears—and——" he suddenly thumped his hand down on the counter. "Wot'm I thinking—o' course I got an advance programme wot me pals sent—'ere y'are, sir——" he fished underneath. "'Ave a look at that—but I'd like it back, if yer don't mind."

The two children and their uncle eagerly leafed through the programme which was handed to them. It was a gaily coloured affair with photographs of the artistes appearing in the circus spread over the centre pages. And given pride of place among them was what they were looking for.

THE GREAT RAMIRO AND HIS WONDERFUL DANCING HORSE. THE MOST AMAZING DISPLAY OF HAUTE ÉCOLE IN THE WORLD!

said the caption. But it was at the photograph that the children gazed. For there was Ramiro in all his elegance mounted on a handsome Arab pony with its foreleg extended in the Spanish Walk. And it wasn't the horse that was in their other photograph. That one had the snow-white coat of age. This was grey—and a mare.

"It's Falla!" breathed Jane, with a little catch in her breath.

The coffee stall proprietor, who had just finished serving customers, leant over his counter in a confidential way again.

"That there's a good act—the dancing 'orse——" he nodded at the photograph. "Been with the boss a good many years. Spanish bloke. Yoo-nique if yer ask me."

They gave back the programme and thanked the little fat man profusely.

"Bit of luck, meeting him!" said Jeremy as they drove out of the town. "What are the plans now, then, Uncle Leslie?"

"Well, you might as well get a visit to the circus out of this affair! What do you say to bringing Storm over next Saturday and exchanging him with Falla after the show?"

Jeremy was struggling with a deep thought.

"Uncle Leslie, won't Ramiro have made a contract or something to appear with the circus for the whole tour? He wouldn't be able to do it with an untrained horse. Perhaps he won't want to part with Falla."

"This time I'm afraid he'll have to," said their uncle firmly. "Even though it means breaking his contract. But I don't think there'll be any trouble. The Toral family always trained stallions for their *haute école* work, and kept the mares for breeding. He might try asking to keep Falla for the rest of the season, but if we say it's now or never for the stallion there won't be any fuss."

"Are you going to tell Ramiro before next Saturday?" asked Jane.

"No," said their uncle. "For one thing I expect he's on the move by now—probably rehearsing Falla with the circus. And for another, I think perhaps it'd be better to spring it on him. It's just a feeling I've got."

Jane nodded. She knew about feelings. She had them herself.

"We must fix up about a horse-box to take Storm over," Uncle Leslie went on.

"Mr. Hutchinson!" said the children together.

"But it'll mean telling him," Jeremy added doubtfully.

"Well, I think we ought to now," said Jane. "He's been awfully kind, and I'd like him to know all about it."

They called in at the farm on the way home and told the kind farmer the whole story. He listened, puffing at his pipe in silence.

"Well, I reckon that's the strangest story I've heard for a long time!" he declared at the end. "And this horse—he hasn't tried to get away?"

"He's as gentle as anything," said Jane. "I think he *wanted* to like people, but no one ap-approved him properly."

"She means 'approached'," explained Jeremy. "But it's quite true. He's come to hand like a lamb."

"It's because he's half Arab," put in Jane. "And everyone knows that Arab horses are nearly human!" She put her hand on Mr. Hutchinson's arm. "You won't tell anyone, will you," she asked. "It's really a secret, and there's only you that knows outside the family."

"Don't you worry yourself, my dear. I won't say a

word!" promised Mr. Hutchinson. "Now, what was the exact arrangement, sir?" he addressed Uncle Leslie.

"I thought the children might bring the horse here early on Saturday and help load him into the horse-box. Then over to Southsea—and we'll follow in my car."

"Couldn't Jeremy and I go in the cab of the lorry?" asked Jane.

"I'm afraid not, Miss Jane. My licence don't cover passengers," explained the farmer. "But the horse'll be safe enough. I've carried plenty of 'em before."

"I'll keep in sight of the box on the way down," promised Uncle Leslie. "That do you, Jane?"

Jane nodded. "And may we bring Storm over some time during the week to introduce him to you and show him the horse-box?" she asked. "He's perfectly all right now, but he likes to get to know things first."

Mr. Hutchinson and Uncle Leslie entered into a technical discussion about distances and prices, while Jeremy and Jane wandered out into the farmyard. The horse-box stood there, and they walked up the sloping ramp made by the dropped tailboard.

"Isn't it lovely to think we'll be bringing Falla back in this!" sighed Jane.

"Another week to wait yet," pointed out Jeremy.

"Oh, that won't take long!" declared Jane. "We can train Storm to the halter and get him used to different things in the evenings."

Even Jane's oddest remarks usually had sense, Jeremy had to admit, because the week didn't "take long"—it just flew by. Uncle Leslie paid a visit to Winchester and arranged the terms of the sale with Mr. Fildred's agent at a price satisfactory to all concerned—in fact near enough to the £70 in notes which had been left in the manger of Falla's shed. Storm was introduced formally to Mr.

Iutchinson and stepped confidently in and out of the horse-ox with Jane at his head after a trial run.

The children were up very early on the Saturday morning. 'hey slipped down to the water meadow before breakfast make sure all was well with Storm, who came up to them ith a friendly whicker.

"I'm rather sorry to be losing him," admitted Jane. "I 'ouldn't part with him for anyone except Falla."

"At least we know he's going to a good master," said eremy comfortingly. "And when he's famous we'll be ble to say that we helped him on his career."

After breakfast they put a halter on the stallion and led im along to Brockenhurst Farm. The horse-box was ready ith a thick bedding of straw, and Storm strode in without a iurmur, accepting nonchalantly the piece of carrot Jane ave him as if he had been travelling all his life.

Mr. Hutchinson fastened up the tailboard and lifted up ane to glance through the little ventilator. Storm was per-ctly at home, pulling contentedly at the hay in a net 'hich they had hung to keep him occupied during the urney.

Mr. Hutchinson started up the lorry and drove out into ie road. The big Lagonda followed up, its engine idling a low speed, and the journey began.

Naturally it took longer than it had done the previous eek, since the speed of the horse-box was considerably ss than that of the Lagonda. They planned to arrive on the eld shortly before the afternoon show started at half past vo. They stopped on Portsdown Hill, overlooking Ports-iouth and Southsea, to eat their sandwiches.

Jane insisted on having Storm out for a nibble at the esh grass—"and a change of air" as she said. Mr. Iutchinson was inclined to refuse, but agreed reluctantly hen Uncle Leslie explained that Storm wouldn't be any trouble. Sure enough, he followed Jane as meekly as an dog.

The farmer scratched his head. "Do seem that Miss Jan can do anything with the horse," he said.

Soon after two o'clock the horse-box was safely parke in a quiet corner of the circus ground. There had certainl been a transformation scene since they were there th previous week—what had been empty ground was now mass of caravans and assorted tents, dominated by the "Bi Top", from which came the sound of many people settlin in their seats for the show.

They had all agreed to see the performance throug before approaching Ramiro. Uncle Leslie had paid a quic visit to the horse lines and assured them that Falla was ther They would have liked to have seen her, but the publ were not allowed in the tent where the horses were stable and they did not want to draw attention to their presenc before it was necessary. In the meantime they settled dow with excitement to enjoy the circus.

Uncle Leslie had got them ringside seats opposite th curtained entrance through which the performers entere the ring.

"Ramiro is the last turn before the interval," said Jerem "Gosh, isn't this fun!"

Then the band struck up, and the circus began. The f man in the coffee stall had been right—it *was* a wonderf show!

There was a troupe of "liberty" horses who trotted roun in the most intricate patterns, changing direction at th ringmaster's voice and the crack of his whip. Jane was little worried at the bearing reins they wore, pulling the chins nearly into their chests.

"It wouldn't be possible to control them running fr with their heads loose," explained Uncle Leslie. "And the only wear them for a short time—it's not as if they had to pull a heavy cart uphill with them on!"

After the horses the trapeze artists, the Flying Foxes, swung effortlessly through the air high above the ring. Jeremy watched with his mouth so wide open that Jane nudged him.

"Shut your mouth, J.," she whispered. "You won't catch one of the Flying Foxes in it—Uncle Leslie says they never fall once they've learnt properly!"

There was a boxing kangaroo that was the funniest thing the children had ever seen. He wore boxing gloves on his front paws, and he bounded round the improvised boxing ring sparring with one of the clowns.

When this was over, there was a fanfare of trumpets and the ringmaster raised his microphone.

"Ladeez and Gentlemen!" came his voice, booming from all round the Big Top. "I now have the honour to present to you the most won-der-ful horse and rider in living memory. Ladeez and Gentlemen . . . Don Ramiro and his world-famous dancing horse!"

The trumpets rang out again, the curtains at the entrance parted, and a horse and rider cantered through and pulled up in one supple movement in the centre of the ring.

The spotlights were trained on the couple as they stood like statues: the rider slim, elegant, faultlessly clad, the horse a wonderful, fairy-tale creature with a proud, arching crest *and the snow-white coat of old age.*

CHAPTER TWELVE

ALMOST A HAPPY ENDING

JEREMY HEARD Jane gasp, and his own heart gave a sickening plunge into his boots. It was Brioso that Ramiro was riding. Why wasn't he on Falla?

He felt his Uncle Leslie's hand on his arm. "Stay here, you two. I'm just going to nip round behind to make sure Falla's all right."

Before Jeremy could answer he was gone like a shadow. Jane half rose as if to follow him, but Jeremy caught hold of her.

"He told us to stay here!" he whispered.

Ramiro had put his horse into a collected canter round the ring as a warming-up exercise, and before he had made more than one circuit their uncle was back.

"She's all right—still tied up in the horse lines," he whispered. "We'll get an explanation afterwards."

Jeremy and Jane relaxed a little, and were able to give their attention to what was going on in the ring. Jane sat forward, her eyes intent.

"It must have been his near shoulder that was hurt," she murmured to Jeremy. "Look—when Ramiro makes him change leg he doesn't keep him more than a couple of strides leading with his left leg."

To someone who understood riding the performance that was being given in the ring was flawless. All the paces were beautifully collected, and the horse and rider moved as one. But the audience as a whole were not riders or horse-lovers. They had come to see what had been billed as a famous dancing horse—not an exhibition of dressage which most of them could not appreciate anyway.

The barracking started in the cheaper seats with an isolated, coarse voice from the back of the tent.

"That ain't no dancin' 'orse," it called. "Come on, Mister. Make 'im dance proper!"

Ramiro did not appear to notice the comment. He completed the last curve of the figure eight and halted the horse. The children could not see the slight movements of hands and legs that gave the office to the horse, but Brioso suddenly broke straight in to the Spanish trot—forelegs extended, hind feet picked up high.

"Lovely!" breathed Jane.

But the movement continued for only a few paces before Ramiro halted the horse again.

"That's more like!" and "Give us some more!" cried the rough voices from the back. Jane pulled at Jeremy's arm.

"Those *beastly* people!" she said. "Look! Brioso's not well—you can see it!"

Brioso hadn't moved since he had been halted after the Spanish trot. He stood like a rock, but the two children could see his sides going in and out with his breathing; and from their ringside seat it was apparent that his neck was rough and grey with sweat.

Suddenly Ramiro slipped from the horse's back. He made a couple of stiff bows to the audience before catching hold of Brioso's bridle and turning to lead him out. The horse followed him, his proud head hanging a little as if he were ashamed—or exhausted. As he passed the ringmaster with his microphone Ramiro threw him a brief word or two.

The man raised the microphone to his mouth as Ramiro and Brioso disappeared through the parted curtains.

"Ladies and Gentlemen . . ." he lowered his microphone

and waited patiently until the shouting and stamping from the back had died down a little. "May I have your attention, *pleez!* Don Ramiro asks me to say that he is unable to perform his act to-day owing to the sudden illness of his horse. We apologise for this unforeseen happening, and ask your indulgence. The show will go on." He pretended complete astonishment as a party of clowns rushed into the ring, carrying him with them, microphone and all, and began an uproarious fooling to cover up the awkward moment.

With one accord the two children followed their uncle this time as he slipped out of the Big Top—nor did he tell them to stay behind. He led them round the maze of vans and lorries at the back of the field to the big marquee that served as the horse lines.

"Your Falla's in there," he told them. "You can go in to her if you like—if anyone tries to stop you say that Ramiro gave you permission!"

"Where're *you* going?" asked Jane.

"To see Ramiro."

"Then can we come too? It isn't that I don't want to see Falla, but I do want to know if Brioso's all right!" Jane's voice trembled a little.

Her uncle hesitated a moment, then nodded.

"All right—come along! But keep in the background, won't you," he said.

They didn't need telling that, and they fell in behind their uncle as he strode over to a big trailer horse-box that stood a little apart from the others.

It was obviously used as a loose-box for Brioso, for the children could hear the noise of a horse being vigorously wisped down, and voices talking in Spanish. Then a small man appeared from the direction of the horse lines staggering under the weight of a bale of straw. He dropped it and proceeded to nip the fastenings before beginning to fork it into the open door of the box.

Jane clutched Jeremy's arm and pulled him behind the big wheels of a nearby trailer.

"That's one of the men who stopped me on Falla!" she whispered. "Look, there's the other! The one who was at the sale!"

Another small dark man had just entered the loose-box with a bucket that gave off a faint steam.

"Bran mash!" said Jeremy, sniffing. "Ramiro's certainly got them running round after him!"

"They don't like it, though," said Jane. "Look at them now!"

The two little dark men were conferring rapidly together outside the box, their faces ugly, with several gestures that looked anything but friendly, in the direction of the doorway.

Then a third figure came hurrying across the grass—a stout, baldish man dressed rather strangely, for the afternoon, in full evening dress.

"Funny clothes to wear," whispered Jane.

"Don't be silly—he's the owner of the circus! He appears in the ring with a top hat at the end of the show!"

"Look—he's going towards the box."

The two Mendozas had melted away at the approach of the proprietor. Nor was there any sign of Uncle Leslie—and he hadn't gone into the box either. But they knew he always had the knack of making himself invisible if he wanted to.

The man in evening dress disappeared inside the horse-box, and a moment later there was an uproar from inside. Suddenly the proprietor appeared in the doorway and came down the ramp at a brisk trot—obviously helped considerably by a push from the rear.

Behind him in the doorway appeared Señor Ramiro Toral

—a slight, dark-clad figure with an air of arrogant dignity.

"You shout in here, it worry my horse," he said quietly. "He is not well—not to shout, please, Mr. Landers."

The proprietor recovered his balance at the foot of the ramp and turned to face the Spaniard. He was not so impressive a figure, but he had a kind of authoritative air of his own.

"All right," he said, his voice quivering. "All right, Don Ramiro. What I've got to say can be said just as well here. And it's that you're finished as far as I'm concerned. Finished! For years I've put up with your bloomin' airs and graces. You had a good act, it was worth it to me. But this is your lot. First of all you play hard to get, then you say your horse is too old and then you give me a story about having a new horse that'll do the act just as well. But when it comes to it, what do you do? Bring in the old crock who can't keep up the pace! Ruin the act! Ruin the show! Why didn't you use the new 'un, eh? Why?"

Ramiro had not moved a muscle during this tirade. When Landers had finally run himself out of breath the Spaniard rolled himself a small thin cigarette with a quick flick of the wrist and lit it.

"I have tell you," he said calmly. "The new horse is *una potranca*—what you call filly, mare, is it not?" He made a scornful gesture. "She do well in training, but for performance in public—no! She is not sensible—her mind is on other things. She is . . . female! And female is only half a horse. I think perhaps I send her back where she comes from."

Jane turned to Jeremy—but Landers had got his breath back by now.

"Ho!" he said. "So you'll send her away. And use that broken-down old nag for the show, eh?"

Ramiro shrugged.

"You speak ignorance, my friend," he said. "Brioso cannot always do all the *haute école* steps because he is old, but every movement he do is perfection. Those who see will appreciate."

"And what sort of audience d'you think I've got? Expert horsemen? Look here, Ramiro . . ."

Jeremy and Jane, listening with all their ears, suddenly realised that Landers was not as angry as he made out. He did not want Ramiro to go, in spite of the trouble he caused.

Looking at the slight, confident figure of Ramiro Toral, Jeremy could dimly understand. There was something about the man—an air of integrity—that made one feel proud to know him. Jeremy shook the thought off. "He's dishonest," he told himself, but his thought answered itself: "No, he isn't—he's honest, but it's his own special kind of honesty!"

"And another thing!" Landers had got up steam again. "Another thing—I don't like those two characters you've got round you, Mendoza or whatever they call themselves. Shifty couple they are. They won't do you or me any good."

Ramiro trod out the butt of his cigarette carefully. Then he turned and glanced into the horse-box behind him. Satisfied that his horse was comfortable he came in a leisurely way down the ramp.

"They are finish. I get rid of them," he said calmly. "And I do the act with Brioso for this season, no?"

"NO!" said Landers explosively. "See here——"

But the Spaniard merely nodded as if Landers had agreed with him and strolled off nonchalantly. "I rest in my van," he threw over his shoulder.

Landers took a deep breath, opened his mouth—and then suddenly seemed to deflate. He scratched his head, disarranging his carefully oiled hair.

"I quite agree—he is a problem," said a voice from the shadow of the horse-box, and Uncle Leslie stepped out.

"How do you do, Mr. Landers," he went on, holding out his hand. "My name is Charter—Leslie Charter."

For a second Landers seemed about to climb on his dignity again, then something in Leslie's friendly grin made him change his mind.

"Charter. Oh, yes, you wrote to me, Mr. Charter," he said. "I remember now."

"And you wouldn't tell me definitely whether Ramiro was in the show or not—because you were considering turning him down?" said Leslie gently.

After a moment's hesitation Landers nodded.

"True enough," he said. "Really, sir, he's getting beyond a joke! Did you hear him just now—reckons the public ought to like his act because it's perfect as far as it goes! I ask you! Trouble is, he's not a showman—he's an artist. And so damn' pleased with himself as well!" The man looked worried. "I don't know why I don't just kick him out. Losing my grip or something, I am."

"No, you're not. I understand perfectly—don't forget I've known him a long time, and his family as well," said Leslie. "But tell me, Mr. Landers—I'm not mistaken when I think you want him with the act as it was before?"

"No question about that! Biggest draw we had, that act was. Never seen anything like that Brioso in his prime. Reckon I was lucky to get him then. We used to hit it off pretty well together. But I've got to consider the public, haven't I, sir?"

"You have, indeed," said Leslie. "But perhaps I can help. I understand that the trouble with the new horse is that she's a mare?"

"Yes—he's right against mares. Mind you, he had great hopes of this one. He wrote me a letter saying that she was shaping up well under training—and he fixed this date for the first public show. But when he got to rehearsing her under show conditions—well, she did play up a bit feminine in the ring. Too interested in everything going on, she was. And now he won't even attempt to use her in the show!"

"Well," said Uncle Leslie. "If that's all the trouble is, I think I may have the answer in that horse-box over in the corner of the field."

The children nudged each other delightedly as Uncle Leslie explained briefly about Storm and his relationship to Brioso. When he had finished Landers whistled.

"A stallion sired by Brioso!" he said. "That'll be a pretty valuable horse, sir, even untrained. Worth a fortune trained, I should say."

"Maybe," said Uncle Leslie. "But his value doesn't matter to us. We only want to exchange with the mare he has now. It's a long story—but my nephew and niece are involved. I don't know where they've got to now—they may be with the mare. They—er—have a considerable interest in her."

"We're here, Uncle Leslie!" Jane wriggled out from under the van. "I'm sorry we were listening, but we didn't think you'd mind, because it was about us and Falla anyway."

Mr. Landers' eyes popped a bit at their sudden appearance but he seemed to accept them and gave them a friendly nod as they were introduced.

"Well, sir, if you'll forgive my hurrying you, shall we fetch Ramiro to see this horse? I've got to be back for the end of the show——"

"Can Jeremy and I go in and see Falla, please?" said Jane to the circus proprietor.

"That's all right," said Mr. Landers, and Uncle Leslie added: "Run along then. I'll fetch you later."

Neither of the children regretted missing the rest of the circus. They felt that the conversations they had overheard provided as good a show as any that was going on inside the Big Top.

"Half a horse he called her!" said Jane indignantly. "I know that's what we say, because she's half yours and half mine, but he's saying she's not good enough for him!"

"Don't let it worry you—she's good enough for us! And how!" said Jeremy feelingly as they entered the horse lines.

All the liberty horses were there, fastened with check reins to the posts of their temporary stalls, facing outwards so they could easily be brought out for their act. Falla was right at the far end, fastened similarly, though she was not saddled.

"Falla!" called Jane, her voice breaking. "Oh, Falla!"

The mare's ears pricked up, and she lifted her head with a shrill whinny at the sound of Jane's voice, and the next moment they were by her side.

A horse cannot exactly smile, or burst into tears of joy as Jane did. But Falla certainly did everything in her power to express her delight at seeing Jeremy and Jane again. When Jane clasped arms round her neck she turned her head and blew lovingly into Jane's ear—and then thrust her nose into Jeremy's pocket to find the piece of carrot he usually had there.

"She remembers everything!" said Jane proudly. "Look, she's doing her little dance!"

Sure enough, Falla was performing the see-saw movement that she had always done when she was particularly proud of herself.

The two children grinned at one another—large, delighted grins. They could hardly believe that their troubles were over and they had their beloved horse again.

"D'you think we could take her out to meet Storm?" suggested Jane.

"Better not—Mr. Landers might not——" Jeremy was eginning. Then he suddenly checked.

"That's funny," he said. "Look—surely that's Mr. Iutchinson's horse-box over there?"

Jane left Falla for a moment and peered out through the :nt flap, which was tied loosely without being quite closed.

The horse-box in which Storm had travelled had been arked in a corner of the field which was clearly visible from iis end of the marquee. But now it wasn't parked any more. t was moving, and as the children watched it reached the orn track leading to the main road and accelerated slightly.

"There's something wrong!" gasped Jeremy. "Did you :e—the two men in the cab were those Mendoza men, I saw iem quite clearly! And Storm's still inside!"

"We must tell Uncle Leslie—quick!" cried Jane, but she poke to empty air.

For Jeremy had wriggled through the gap in the opening f the tent, emerging rather like a cork from a bottle. Then e was haring across the grass towards the horse-box, which ad stopped at the entrance to the field waiting for a chance › pull out into the steam of traffic.

And then the horrified Jane saw him reach the lorry, atch hold of the edge of the raised tailboard, and swing imself on to the back of the van, where he balanced preariously with one foot on the projecting metal hinges, linging like a limpet.

Before she could move or call out the lorry found a gap ı the traffic and roared off to the right, with Jeremy hanging n for grim death behind.

CHAPTER THIRTEEN

JEREMY IS A HERO

JEREMY DID not see Jane crawl out of the tent flap and te
across to find Uncle Leslie. He was far too busy cor
centrating on his precarious hold.

Luckily the road was smooth, and as the van gathere
speed he was able to wriggle into a safer position with bot
his feet anchored. He realised with a sinking heart th
there was no chance of his being able to get inside th
horse-box, since the tailboard when it was up secured th
door. He would have to stay stuck on the back.

The progress of the lorry along the sea front did not g
unmarked. Many of the passers-by saw Jeremy clingin
on at the back, and there were angry and alarmed cries a
the lorry passed. But until the lorry had gone by Jerem
could not be noticed and none of these noises reached th
men in the front cab.

Now they were leaving the populous area and were ou
on the open road. The lorry picked up speed. Jeremy trie
to find a more comfortable grip, but the lorry swerved t
pass a cyclist and he nearly lost his hold altogether. He fe
sick for a moment, but he managed to cling on again.

They had been going for about twenty minutes by now
and Jeremy's hands were fast losing any feeling. He kne
it was only a question of time before his fingers would g
completely numb and lose their grip. He looked down an
caught a glimpse of the road rushing by below him an
hastily looked back again.

His fingers were opening slowly . . . slowly. With a sob he wedged one elbow into the gap between the tailboard and the door, which left him free to detach one hand. It was horribly painful since the movement of the lorry closed the gap as the tailboard shifted, and his elbow felt as if it were being crushed. He flexed his fingers frantically, trying to get some feeling back into them.

It was no use, he thought. He would have to let go. He counted up to ten. He was feeling rather dizzy now. He tried to count ten more.

But as he got to "five" of the second ten the lorry swung right-handed through an open gate, bumped up a narrow track for a few yards, then turned again and stopped.

Jeremy fell off rather than got off, and simply collapsed in a heap on the ground. But he knew he would be discovered if he stayed there, and the thought gave him the strength to move. He couldn't walk, but he crawled as rapidly as he could away from the lorry. And chance rather than design led him to the shelter of a small shed that stood at the side of the farmyard in which the lorry had stopped. He was only just in time. He pulled his second foot inside the door as the lorry doors were slammed shut and the two Mendoza brothers appeared behind the lorry.

Jeremy was lying on the ground inside the shed, hardly daring to breathe. He had not had time to push the door to, but he was well behind it, and he found that there was a knot-hole in the wood just near the ground which he could see through.

The two men were talking in low voices, and Jeremy could see that they were unfastening the tailboard of the horse-box. They lowered it, and opened the doors, and one of them—the taller—entered.

Jeremy heard Storm give a shrill whinny, then there was a wild scuffling of hooves. The man appeared in the doorway again, backing hurriedly down the ramp, his swarthy face yellow with fear.

The smaller man made some short sharp comment in Spanish, then he advanced himself up the ramp. Jeremy pricked up his ears. The man was making Jane's chirruping noise—but the one she had made that night she had caught Storm, the one she did not remember having made.

Then the man disappeared inside the horse-box, and came out again leading Storm by his halter—and Storm was following him as meekly as a lamb.

Over the other side of the yard was a big barn with double doors, which now stood open. It was obviously used to store the farm machinery. And outside stood another horse-box facing towards a gate at the other end of the farmyard.

Jeremy could see what they were going to do, as clearly as if he understood what they were saying. They intended to transfer Storm to the other horse-box and abandon the one they had stolen!

Sure enough, the smaller brother led Storm easily into the second vehicle, and the two men shut the doors and put up the tailboard.

Jeremy lay in the shed feeling more helpless and miserable than he ever remembered feeling in his life. He knew wha would happen now—they would just get in and drive off drive off with Storm, and no doubt sell him for a handsome figure . . . probably disguise him first in some way . . Jeremy remembered that Uncle Leslie had said they were experienced in doubtful horse-dealing. And he, Jeremy just had to lie there, completely unable to stop them.

He watched hopelessly through the gap on the hinged side of the shed door, waiting for them to get into the cab of the second lorry. Automatically he noticed its number—GRU 881H. He could tell the police that, anyway.

Then he gave a start. For the two men did not immed

tely get into the horse van. They came back to where ey had left Mr. Hutchinson's van, and one of them got up to the cab while the other walked over to the doorway of e barn and disappeared inside.

With a very faint leap of his heart Jeremy saw that they ere driving the horse-box inside the barn, probably to nceal it and delay its discovery as long as possible.

His brain whirled. A chance . . . did that give him a ance to do something while they were out of view the lorry in the barn? Something that would stop them -prevent the lorry from moving? The tyres—could he ncture them? A glance at the huge thick covers dis-uraged him. It would need something really sharp, ielded with considerable pressure to get through. His out knife? No, he hadn't got that—he had taken it f his belt when Jane caught Storm and hadn't put it back t.

Jeremy glanced desperately round the shed. It was a relict place, with a few empty sacks in one corner, the or sagging on its hinges, the window broken . . . the indow! There was a big sharp jagged piece of glass sticking at the bottom of it! If he could somehow work it loose might penetrate that tyre.

He rose to his feet, and wrapping a handkerchief und his hand began to work cautiously at the broken glass. he faint grating sound it made seemed like a roll of drums Jeremy, and he held his breath while he glanced fearfully er at the barn. But Mr. Hutchinson's lorry and the two en were out of sight for the moment, and he could still ar the engine running—doubtless they were manœuvring e lorry behind other machinery.

Then to his joy the piece of glass broke free from the old tty, and he was left holding a roughly triangular piece, th a jagged point and an edge like a razor.

Jeremy looked over at the barn again. He was still saf
It seemed to him that he had taken hours working the glas
free, but in fact it was only seconds.

He edged cautiously out of the shed and made a quic
crouching dash for the horse-box, and dived underneath i
Once there he breathed a little easier, for he was hidde
from the barn by the big wheels.

He knelt beside one of the huge front tyres and began
cut at it with the glass in his hand. It was surprising
difficult. The rubber was immensely thick, and even th
glass did not seem to cut it very fast.

Suddenly he heard what he had been dreading to hear-
the noise of the engine in the barn had stopped. He realise
it could only be a matter of moments now before the tw
men would appear again. With a half sob he tried to sa
even harder at the tyre, and the glass slipped, cutting deep
into his palm.

He dropped the piece of glass, staring stupidly at th
blood welling from his hand. It didn't hurt—the edge w
too sharp for that—but it looked pretty deep.

Then, working as quickly as he could, and ignoring th
blood dripping from his hand, he wedged the triangular pie
of glass with its point against the massive wheel, and fixed
in position with a couple of stones each side. It was the be
he could do; when the wheel moved its own weight mig
drive the jagged point in—far more strongly than he himse
could ever have done it.

There was no time for more. Even as he wedged the la
stone in he heard the cab doors slam inside the barn. H
glanced quickly behind him, and realised that if he we
careful he could keep the lorry between him and the ba
for the few precious moments it would take him to get o
of the gate and down the farm track leading back to th
road.

He backed cautiously until he reached the safety of the ırning beyond the gateway, and as soon as he was out of ght of the barn he turned and ran like a hare towards the ɔad again.

At the road he stopped, panting, to gather his thoughts ıd work out what to do next. He was conscious of a dull ırobbing in his injured hand, and he looked at it. That was mistake, he realised; the blood was still welling out and ripping off the ends of his fingers, and it made him feel a it sick to see it.

He pulled out his now rather dirty handkerchief and tied round his hand as tightly as he could, pulling the knot rm with his teeth.

Then suddenly he heard a sound—the one he was waiting r! It made him forget his hand—for it was the sound of ıe engine of GRU 881H being started up!

The revs increased as the motor was put into gear, and ırough the still air Jeremy could hear the change of engine ɔte as the clutch was released and the wheels began to ove. Then there was a tremendous bang that scared ıe rooks out of the trees, and the engine choked and opped.

When the echoes of the bang died away all was quiet ;ain, but Jeremy with a grin could imagine the activity ıat was taking place up at the farmyard—jacking up the ıge frame to change the wheel. He did a little war-dance joy.

Then he sobered up. There was still a lot to be done. e must find a telephone box and get hold of the police.

The main road was empty each way as far as he could see -then he blinked his eyes. Surely that was a telephone box hich he could see about fifty yards along? He blinked ;ain. His eyes seemed to be rather misty, somehow and ıere was no doubt about it, he did feel rather wobbly about

the legs. But he gritted his teeth and made what speed h
could towards the phone box.

But as he got nearer he faltered, for there was somethin
wrong. He pressed a hand to his aching head. Oh, ye
of course—phone boxes were usually red, and this one wa
yellow and black. It wasn't an ordinary public telephone,
was one belonging to the A.A., for motorists. Jeremy shoo
his head to try and clear it. Only people who belonged t
the Automobile Association could have a key to open thes
boxes—he remembered his uncle telling them about it.

"I'll have to stop a car," Jeremy thought. "I hope it'
be one that belongs to the A.A. They have a badge on th
front, don't they?"

Because his legs wouldn't hold him any more he sat dow
on the grass by the side of the road. He wished he coul
have a drink of water—he did feel dreadfully thirsty. An
things kept on going funny in front of his eyes . . . but h
could hang on until a car came, he told himself.

Then he heard the roar of a distant engine, and in th
distance appeared a car travelling pretty fast. Jerem
wearily heaved himself to his feet. "Must stop it in goo
time," he muttered.

He staggered out into the middle of the road, and stoo
there, waving his good arm as hard as he could. The drive
saw him, and began to slow down, but it took time at th
speed he was going. Jeremy didn't hear him stop, fo
suddenly things went very misty indeed, and he sat dow
abruptly where he was in the road.

He must have blacked out for the moment, for the nex
thing he knew was a familiar voice saying: "Quick, get th
first-aid kit from the car!"

Jeremy opened his eyes.

"I'm all right," he began.

"Swallow this!" said the voice above his head, an

Jeremy obediently took a mouthful of something that made him choke and gasp, but went down into his stomach like fire and left him feeling decidedly better.

He looked up. No wonder the voice had been familiar! For it was Uncle Leslie—and he could see Jane hopping round anxiously behind. Jeremy clutched at his uncle's arm.

"Uncle Leslie!" he said. "Thank goodness it's you! Quick—they're there—up that farm track. They changed into another horse-box, but I've punctured their tyre . . . but they may have got the wheel changed by now."

The great thing about Uncle Leslie was that he acted first and asked questions afterwards.

"Into the car—quick, all of you!" he said. He picked up Jeremy and dumped him into the back, where he was followed by Jane and—to his surprise—Ramiro! Mr. Hutchinson was there too, but Jeremy had not time to feel anything more, for Uncle Leslie was backing the car rapidly towards the opening of the farm track.

"Keep that hand of yours up, Jeremy," he said over his shoulder. And as he spoke he stopped, changed gear, and shot forward and up the track.

"Do hurry," Jeremy implored him quite unnecessarily. "Don't *fuss*, Jane. I'm all right. They'll be——"

He stopped, for even above the sound of the car they were in he could hear the deep roar as the engine of GRU 581H started up. And as they turned the last corner into the farmyard they saw the back of the lorry disappearing in a cloud of dust as it went out through the other gate and up the cart track.

Uncle Leslie didn't even slow down. He just swung the Lagonda straight round and through the gate, following behind the lorry.

"I'm afraid they've spotted us," he said between his

teeth. "They're increasing speed—but they can't get away."

"I wish they'd stop!" cried Jane. "It's dangerous going as fast as that on this bumpy track—especially with Storm in the box."

Jeremy blinked. He felt rather as if he were floating two feet above everyone else, and things were decidedly unreal. For a moment he even wondered if he were dreaming, then a larger bump than usual jolted his cut hand, and he realised that it was all true.

He watched the horse-box swaying in front of them along the rough track—swaying dangerously. And suddenly he was in the middle of a nightmare—a nightmare about a horse-box travelling too fast through the New Forest . . . a crash . . . the splintering of wood . . . shrill whinnies of pain and fear . . . and a still body by the side of the road.

He shook his head sharply. Of course it wasn't true. GRU 881H was still careering along in front of them; everything was still all right.

And then suddenly it wasn't. For the over-driven horse-box had struck an extra deep rut in the hard surface. It swerved, and struck another one. Completely out of control it shot right off the track and went crashing through the hedge at the side.

Jeremy shut his eyes. He couldn't help it—here was his nightmare coming true! He heard Jane give a stifled scream, heard the sound of breaking branches—and then silence.

CHAPTER FOURTEEN

A HAPPY ENDING AFTER ALL

JEREMY HAD his eyes closed for only a fraction of a second. He opened them again in silence—and saw the horse-ox in front of them, its bonnet flat up against a tree trunk ie whole thing slightly askew . . . but still the right 'ay up!

The next moment all was activity. Uncle Leslie had 'opped the car and was out like a flash. Ramiro from the 'ont seat was with him, and Jane beat the slower Mr. Iutchinson by yards.

Ramiro and Jane made straight for the back of the van, id Ramiro started unfastening the tailboard. And now eremy could hear furious squeals and thumps from inside—bviously Storm was showing his disapproval of such rough 'eatment.

It did not take long for Ramiro to get the tailboard wered, but before he could do more Jane was up it like flash and had opened the doors of the box. Jeremy could ear her chirruping to the horse, and the noises quietened : once. Ramiro followed her in, and after a few moments iey appeared again, one on each side of Storm as he stepped irefully down the sloping ramp.

In the meantime Uncle Leslie and Mr. Hutchinson had one round to the cab and were pulling out the Mendoza rothers. They did not seem to be badly hurt, just con-derably shaken, and the one that had been driving was leeding from a cut lip. Uncle Leslie spoke a word to Ir. Hutchinson, who nodded and came back to the car.

"I'm going back to phone for the police," he said to Jeremy. "Are you coming too, Master Jeremy?"

Jeremy shook his head. "I want to see what's going on," he said, climbing out of the car.

Mr. Hutchinson backed the car to a gateway at the side of the track, turned, and roared off back to the farm and the road. Jeremy sat down on the grass bank, content to be a spectator.

The two Mendozas were obviously not going to cause any more trouble. They sat side by side, one dabbing at his cut lip occasionally, with all the fight knocked out of them.

Jeremy transferred his attention to Ramiro and Jane, who were going carefully all over Storm for cuts or damage of any kind.

"He's not hurt at all," declared Jane, straightening up. "Golly, that's lucky, isn't it, Mr. Ramiro?" She came round to the same side as the Spaniard and squatted companionably on the ground beside him. "You'll like him," she went on. "When you feed him you'll find he blows his oats round the manger. It's a little wasteful, but it keeps him awfully happy while he picks up all the odd bits. Falla does it too—but I expect you know that." She suddenly stopped and frowned. "We thought it was dreadful of you to take Falla away from us," she told him. "We were so miserable. Imagine how you'd feel if someone took Brioso!"

Ramiro looked at her in silence for a moment, and Jeremy wondered whether he was going to be offended. Then the Spaniard's glance softened, and he smiled—a gentle charming smile that altered his whole face. He held out his hand to Jane.

"I did not at first think it was wrong," he said. "But now I am in great sorrow to have made you unhappy. I hope you will forgive."

Jane only hesitated a second before placing her hand in his.

Uncle Leslie came over to Jeremy and jerked his head towards Jane and Ramiro, who were talking together animatedly now.

"A love of horses is a great thing in common," he said. "Now, how are you feeling?"

"Fine!" declared Jeremy, not quite truthfully. "Shall I come and show you where they put Mr. Hutchinson's horse-box? It's in the barn back there."

Uncle Leslie took a look at Jeremy's rather white face and pressed him down again gently.

"You've done your share—and a bit more," he said. "Take it easy for a bit now." He picked up Jeremy's hand and examined the blood-soaked handkerchief.

"It's stopped bleeding for the moment," he went on. "But we must get you down to a doctor as soon as we can and have it looked at."

At that moment Mr. Hutchinson drove back from the phone box.

"Police'll be here in about ten minutes, sir," he said. Then added to Jeremy, "What a game! I wasn't gone more'n a minute, back at the circus ground. Those two furriners must a' been waiting, and took their chance. Luckily Miss Jane had seen the way they went, and there was only the one main road, so we followed 'em up. But if it hadn't been for you, young Jeremy, we'd have missed them for sure when they turned off the road."

The police were as good as their word, and a squad car turned up as they got back to the farmyard.

Statements and name and addresses were taken all round, and before long the two Mendoza brothers were hustled into the back of the car and borne away.

"Are they going to prison?" asked Jeremy.

"I should think so," said Uncle Leslie grimly. "I've found out some things about those two gentlemen recently, besides the spot of bother they're in now—and I'll have some evidence ready before the case comes up."

"Good!" declared Jane. "Serve them right for doping Jeremy!" She leant through the Lagonda window—Jeremy had been ordered by his uncle to stay in the car. "J., how are you feeling? I've been neglecting you rather, but I was talking to Mr. Ramiro. He's awfully interesting!"

"So I noticed," said Jeremy. Then relenting, as Jane's face fell a little. "All right, Janey. Actually I think he's a pretty fine chap, and what's more I know Uncle Leslie does too!"

Ramiro and Jane helped to get Storm loaded back into Mr. Hutchinson's horse van. In spite of his "no passenger" rule the farmer took Ramiro and Jane in the cab with him. To say "No" to someone like Ramiro was apparently beyond his powers, and Jane was not to be parted from her new Spanish friend.

Uncle Leslie and Jeremy drove back to the circus ground together. They were lucky enough to find a doctor's surgery open on the way, and in spite of Jeremy's protests he was taken in. The doctor gave him an anti-tetanus injection straight away, and put a couple of stitches into the cut on his hand.

"You can go to your own doctor to have those out in a week's time," he told Jeremy. "You're lucky—an inch lower and it would have been the artery, and you wouldn't be here now!"

"Could I have a drink?" asked Jeremy. "I feel awfully thirsty."

The doctor gave him a sharp glance. "Lost a bit of blood I should imagine," he said. He went away and came back with a tall glass filled with some pink fluid that fizzed. "Drink it all," he said. "It'll make you feel better."

Jeremy did as he was told, though it wasn't very nice. But it did make him feel better—in fact things came back into focus after being rather fuzzy round the edges, and he began to take an intelligent interest again.

When they arrived back at the fairground Jane was waiting at the entrance.

"Mr. Hutchinson's gone on back with Falla because he goes slower than we do," she reported. "If we're not back he's promised to put her in the water meadow for us. I wanted to wait for you—you have been a long time!"

Uncle Leslie explained about the doctor, and Jeremy, who was feeling quite different after the pink fizzy drink, got out of the car, and followed Jane and his uncle over to Ramiro's quarters. The Spaniard was waiting at the door of his caravan to greet them.

"May we go over and say good-bye to Storm first," said Jane. Ramiro nodded his permission, and Jane led the way to the second travelling loose box where Storm was stabled. She stroked the horse's velvety nose and ran her hand lovingly down his strong neck.

"Good-bye, you beauty," she whispered.

When they returned to the caravan their uncle was talking to Mr. Landers, and as the children came up they heard Uncle Leslie say:

"Well—what do you think about it all?"

Landers gave an exaggerated shrug, but he could not hide the big grin on his face.

"Looks as though I'm saddled with the old devil again," he said happily. "Between you and me, sir, I'll be glad to have him back, trouble though he is. Beats me, but there you are!"

Ramiro returned at that moment—he had been giving Brioso his feed—and Jane went to his side.

"Mr. Ramiro, you *will* promise to write to us when you have got your new horse trained so that we can come and see you in the circus?" she asked.

"You have my word for to do so," said Ramiro gravely.

Then it was time to go and Jeremy and Jane walked back slowly to the gate, their uncle following, deep in conversation with Ramiro.

Farewells were said all round, and the children got in the car. But just as they were about to move off Jane leant forward from the back seat and clutched her uncle's arm.

"Don't go for just a moment, Uncle Leslie!" she implored. "There's something I've forgotten! Wait for me—I'll only be a second!"

She got out of the car and ran over to where Ramiro stood, waiting to wave good-bye. The others saw her stand on tiptoe to ask him a question. They saw him smile and bend down to whisper an answer in her ear. Then she came back and climbed into the car again.

"What was that you asked Ramiro?" said Jeremy as they drove out of the fairground entrance.

"I asked him what he was going to call the new horse," said Jane. "And he told me!"

She paused, and Jeremy said: "Well—go on—tell us too!"

"*Afortunado!*" she burst out. "It means 'Fortunate' in Spanish—and it's after us! Fortune—Afortunado! Isn't it wonderful?"

"Good for Ramiro!" agreed their uncle. "I reckon it's no more than you both deserve, too!"